Puss Food

AND OTHER JAMAICAN STORIES

Ditta Sylvester

LMH PUBLISHING LIMITED

Editors: Tyrone S. Reid and Kenisha T. Duff
Cover illustration: Courtney Lloyd Robinson
Cover design: Sanya Dockery
Typeset & book layout: Sanya Dockery

Published by: LMH Publishing Limited
Suite 10-11
Sagicor Industrial Park
7 Norman Road
Kingston C.S.O., Jamaica
Tel.: (876) 938-0005; Fax: (876) 759-8752
Email: lmhbookpublishing@cwjamaica.com
Website: www.lmhpublishing.com

Printed in the U.S.A

ISBN: 978-976-8202-79-6

NATIONAL LIBRARY OF JAMAICA CATALOGUING IN PUBLICATION DATA

Sylvester, Ditta

    Puss food and other Jamaican stories / Ditta Sylvester
    p. ; cm.
ISBN 978-976-8202-79-6 (pbk)

1. Short stories, Jamaican   2. Jamaican fiction

I. Title

813   - dc 22

CONTENTS

TO DIE OR NOT TO DIE

"Dinna ready," Maud Jackson told her children.

The three kids and their mother assembled around the little dining table and began the meal of stew peas and rice.

"Clear di table and wash up, Ruth," Miss Maud said after they had finished eating. "Willard, go get some fire wood afta you bring in di goat dem."

"Keith can come help mi?" the boy asked.

"You too lazy!" his mother shouted. "Dat a nuh nutten fi a big boy like you manage. You well know say yuh likkle bredda delicate."

"Yes, Mama," Willard said.

"Hurry up wid wha you doin', Ruth!" her mother urged. "Memba you haffi done and come bathe Keith."

But him big enough fi bathe himself! Ruth wanted to say. Instead she said, "Yes, Mama."

Keith was the 'wash belly'. Six years after his birth, Maud decided that Keith would be her last baby. Thus, much of the attention which was rightly due to his older siblings was diverted to him, and he lapped it up like a selfish little puppy.

His brother and sister began to see him as an intruder who had barged into their little family with the sole purpose of stealing their mother's love. But these feelings had to be kept carefully hidden. They were compelled by their mother to be constantly loving and protective of their "little brother".

Keith was in his thirties when Miss Maud died. Willard, the oldest, and Ruth had moved out years ago to start work and relationships of their own. Much of what they earned they contributed to the maintenance of Keith and their mother, since Keith was too lazy to work and their mother was not strong enough. Fortunately, the small house in which they lived had been owned by their long deceased father.

Now alone in the house, Keith was beginning to get depressed. He never for a moment entertained the thought that his siblings had also been affected by their mother's passing. Though they still continued to care for him financially and otherwise, he felt neglected and began to toy with the idea of killing himself. He was much less concerned about hurting himself than he was about paying back his siblings for not lavishing upon him the attention he figured he so richly deserved.

When neighbours stopped to enquire how he was doing, Keith told them he was doing very poorly, since his mother's passing had left him all alone in the world, and that his siblings' neglect had also severely affected him. Then he would declare with much resignation and self-pity that his suffering would not last much longer since he was soon to join his dearly departed mother.

At first, no one took these remarks seriously. Keith eventually picked up on this and decided to remedy the situation. He wrote a letter telling everyone that he could not go on living, and because he now had no one, he felt compelled to put an end to his miserable existence. Then, leaving the letter in a place where his brother was sure to find it, he took off carrying a length of rope.

The letter was discovered about an hour later, and the whole community went in search of their errant son. Climbing the hill to his Golgotha had made Keith very tired, so he decided to take a quick nap on a pile of banana trash, which lay in the shade of a big mango tree. When he was properly rested, he told himself that he would carry out the dastardly though necessary deed. Moments later, Willard and his friends found him asleep with the rope in his hand.

Overcome with joy and relief, Willard and Ruth showered their brother with more love and attention than he had ever known. Keith was very happy. Then it dawned on him: This was the way to keep them on their toes! Whenever they fell short, he would threaten to kill himself. And this he did for several years. Keith Jackson never ceased to exhaust and frighten everybody who cared about him with constant threats of suicide.

Keith came home late from church one evening in a bad mood. He had been living with his sister and her husband for some time. Since his mother's passing, Sister Lurline always seemed to be present somewhere along the borders of his life. By now, he had become practised in the art of keeping her and the other single hopefuls in the church at bay. But she was making herself so obvious nowadays, it was hard to ignore her. She looked nice, but who told her he was seeking a wife? He couldn't even take care of himself!

As was his habit, Keith leaned against the big stone at the corner of the house to eavesdrop on Ruth and her husband, Joe. He had to keep up to date with what they were thinking.

"Is a pity him cyaan dead meck wi bury him!"

That was his sister's voice. But who was she talking about? It had to be Joe. Keith had been hoping for a long time that something would happen for them to break up. Their closeness made him feel left out. Now it seemed something finally had. He smiled to himself. He was listening to hear who Ruth was complaining to about her husband, when he heard Joe say:

"Shame o' you, Ruth! You own likkle bredda? You don't mean dat!"

Keith wanted to run, but he only managed to stand upright.

"Likkle bredda? Likkle bredda?" Ruth said derisively. "Him don't little again, an' I cant put up wid him anymore. Him a kill mi, man!"

"But you suppose to use to him by now," Joe said.

"If you did know him as long as me," Ruth replied, "you woulda tired a him to."

"So is funeral you want now?"

"Betta him dead an' go to Mum," said Ruth. "Is only she him care 'bout."

Keith Jackson could hardly believe his ears. His own sister wanted him dead. What hold did he have over her now? Quietly, he wept in the darkness. His tears seemed at odds with the cool quiet of the night. Suddenly, being dead became a very unattractive prospect.

Silently, Keith went into the house and crawled into bed. For many hours he lay awake trying to come up with a plan to get back at his sister and all his enemies who wanted him dead. But how? Shortly before he fell asleep, he came to the conclusion that this idea of suicide had to be put on hold, at least for the time being.

⚶

Joe greeted Keith cheerfully the following morning as they sat down to their usual big breakfast. Throughout the meal, he stared in wonder at Keith. For the first time since he had come to live with them, he was eating heartily without even criticizing the food. He seemed hardly aware of Joe's presence.

As the days passed, Keith began to put on weight and became stronger. Everybody except him was pleased. He decided that since his death would prove convenient for some people, he would be a fool to oblige them. He was going to live! He would show them. He would show them that he was not somebody to be trifled with. Keith Jackson was nobody's fool! He would show them that he could do just about anything he set his mind to.

And he did.

Over the next few weeks, Keith threw himself into farming. He planted bananas and red peas. He reared goats and chickens. He even managed to start a small business. Then he married Sister Lurline. He forgot to pay too much attention to himself and fell head over heels, deep in love, with his new wife.

Years later, he became the father of two daughters and a son, they became the centre of his life. He worked hard at educating them well and showered them with love. His daughters grew up, got married and gave him three grandchildren. And when he got older, his son took over the family business.

Keith now spends most of his time at home. Ruth, now widowed, lives with him. She is very proud of her "little brother," but she still teases him from time to time.

"So when you plannin' to go to Mum?" she asks him one afternoon.

" Don't rush mi, Ma'm, don't rush mi!" Keith responds with a roar of laughter. "Is funeral you want?"

"Is Joe did say dat!" Ruth laughs. "Him was a good man."

"Yes," Keith agrees. "A kind man. Him an' Willard."

"Dem two woulda tek anybody talkin' bout committin' suicide very serious you know, Keith? If I did know you was listenin', I wouldn't did say dem tings dat night at all!"

"But if I did know you was goin' to say dem tings, I wouldn't did a listen!"

Ruth smiles.

"Me an' you will soon be joinin' Joe an' Willard an' Mum now," she said. "What a way time fly!"

"Listen, Ruth," replies Keith, "speak for youself, you hear? I have no intention of gettin' myself mix up wid no dead people right now. I plan to live till everybody begin to wonder if mi goin' to dead at all!"

From her kitchen, Lurline Jackson hears her husband and sister-in-law and wonders if it is possible for somebody to die laughing. Maud Jackson had not died laughing. It had been the woman's own fault, holding on to Keith like nobody but herself should have him! Well, the old woman had learnt her lesson the hard way. Lurline remembered the day Miss Maud had dared to tell her that Keith was too good for a little nobody like her. Old witch! They had all assumed Maud had died of a heart attack but...

Lurline looked through the kitchen window at Keith and his sister. Yes, he was happy, she thought; and so were they all. She grinned. *Who has the last laugh now, Maud Jackson?* Ruth was nothing like her mother. She enjoyed her brother's company but was not overly possessive. Lurline sighed and smiled to herself. She hoped things would remain the way they were.

Because, if not, somebody else would have to die.

THE WIDOW'S MIGHT

When Donna's husband died, everybody said it was a shame for such a young woman to become a widow. Derrick had met her at the local beauty shop where she worked. Donna had just left her mother's home to work in Glandon with Mrs. Black, the owner of the shop. He had come in just to pass the time and had been instantly attracted to the pretty, hard-working young woman.

Derrick was a big man about town. He had been raised by his maternal grandmother, who had passed away some years ago. Charming and determined, he had become quite a successful businessman. He had been a 'girly-girly' man, but felt it was time to quit his womanizing ways and settle for the respectability of married life.

Donna insisted on a small wedding. Only Judith the bride's mother; Judith's aunt, Alice; and a few other relatives attended. The rest of the party had been made up of a few of Derrick's close friends. After the honeymoon, the couple moved into a big, new house that Derrick had recently bought in the suburbs of Glandon. Donna reluctantly agreed to quit working and completely devoted herself to the business of caring for home and husband.

Even before the birth of the couple's first child, Derrick had begun to find the confines of marriage much too restricting. At first, his infidelities were discreet but by the birth of their second, he was enjoying himself too much to be careful. That which God had "joined together" was fast beginning to unravel.

Their second baby was almost two when a new lady doctor came to town. Later that same week, Derrick paid her a visit. He fell in love instantly and was prompt in keeping the appointment for his second visit. The doctor ushered him gently into her office and, with more kindness and concern than he had ever experienced, informed him that he was HIV positive.

When his wife and children came home that night, Derrick was found hanging by his neck from a rafter in the ceiling.

Not many days after he was buried, Donna discovered, to her dismay, that her late husband was not the great businessman everybody thought he was. She had felt compelled by relatives and friends to give him a huge, expensive funeral if only to detract attention from the manner in which he had died. Now she had no money and would shortly have to leave the heavily mortgaged house. Donna was shocked to find out that her legacy was little more than a mite. She had no choice but to return to work.

Mrs. Black was more than happy to have her back, and old customers at the beauty shop showered her with sympathy and compassion. But for some strange reason, no one wanted her to do their hair. By the end of her first day, Donna felt totally rejected and wondered what she had done wrong. That night she spoke to Mrs. Black, who was concerned but seemed to have no answers. She suggested that Donna might have better luck if she did nails the following day.

At about eleven o'clock, a stylishly dressed young woman came in for a manicure. As Donna proceeded with the job, the woman said, "I'm sure I have seen you before, but I just can't place you. Are you new here?" She spoke with an accent.

"I did work here a few years ago," Donna told her. "But mi stop an' come back yesterday."

"You left to have a baby?" the woman asked.

"Two baby an' a funeral."

"What?! Who died?"

"Mi husban'."

"You talking about that big funeral two weeks ago?" the customer asked.

Donna confirmed that it was.

"Derrick's funeral?" the woman continued.

Donna looked up. "You did know him?" she asked.

The woman looked away, chuckling quietly. "Did I know him," she said, almost to her herself. "So you were Derrick's wife," she continued after a pause. "I should have known!"

"What you mean by dat?" Donna asked suspiciously.

"Nothing."

Minutes passed and Donna continued working on the woman's nails. Then, without warning, the young woman pulled her hand away and stood up abruptly.

"Is what?" Donna asked, surprised.

"I have to go."

"But mi not finish," Donna said. "You leavin' wid two nails not done?"

"They say you can't get it by touching," the woman said, "but I not too sure about that!"

"What you talking about?" Donna asked, confused.

The woman gave her a long, knowing look and said, "I know why Derrick killed himself."

So that was it, Donna thought to herself. That was why everybody was avoiding her touch. They all believed that Derrick had given her the virus. The thought had occurred to her, but she had refused to face it. Now it had come back like a slap. She stared into the silence, which was soon broken by the clip-clop of the woman's heels on the pavement outside.

"Road-runna Jean dat!" Mrs. Black said crisply.

"Who?" Donna asked.

"Jean. Because she so up an' dung all over dis worl', she believe say she betta dan everybody!"

"Oh…But is who she?"

"You don't want to know," Mrs. Black answered. "Come. I goin' to pay you fi dis week. Stay home an' res' youself till nex' week you come back."

Donna thanked her and left, knowing fully well that there would be no point in returning to work there.

Days later, Donna was presiding over a rather unattractive stall in the town's market. Sure it was a step down, but her children had to eat. Her small assortment of slippers, under-wear and children's clothes was quickly depleted, and she was beginning to feel better. She had just returned from replenishing her stock one afternoon, when she detected a change in the atmosphere. It was tense. Everybody seemed on edge. She suddenly felt the need to visit the bathroom, so she asked the neighbouring vendor to watch her stall.

When she got back, most of her goods were lying on the floor of the market, while the other vendor tried to bury her face deeper into the newspaper she was pretending to read. Fear, like the cold hand of death, held and crippled Donna for a moment. She felt like a cornered mouse. In a daze, she gathered her things from the floor and began to pack up for the day.

Nervously, she made her way out of the market. Donna wished with all her heart that she could make herself invisible. She was approaching the gate of the market when she heard someone shout, "AIDS gal!"

She stopped and looked back. Nobody looked at her, but she could feel the tension. She turned and continued walking, wondering what would happen next. She was almost through the gate and was about to breathe a sigh of relief, when she felt a stone hit her on the back followed by shouts of:

"Dutty gal!"

"AIDS gal!"

"We nuh want nuh AIDS from you!"

"Come out yah!"

Donna's feet took on a life of their own, and she ran as fast as she could. When she finally stopped, she realized that she was in front of the cemetery on the outskirts of the town. She was surprised to find that she was still clutching her bag of goods. Donna sat on a stone and put her face in her hands. She cried long and loud like a lost and frightened child. It was dark when her feet dragged her home.

When morning broke, she fed the children cornmeal porridge, got them dressed and told them this was the day they would be visiting their grandma in the country. The three arrived at their destination before noon. Her mother, Judith, was surprised but happy to see them. When they were alone, she asked, "So what really bring you here today?"

Judith's heart ached as she listened to what had happened. They hugged and cried and talked and prayed together. And Judith tried her hardest to talk her daughter out of what Donna was planning to do next.

"I goin' somewhere down di country," she told her. "Maybe I coulda go down by Aunt Alice. Mi have to find a little place to continue wid mi hair dressin' an' sellin'."

"But why you have to go now?" Judith asked. "Stay here wid mi a little. You been through hell. Give youself a little time, man."

"Mama, di longer I stay here di harder it will be fo' mi to leave again. You alone can't provide for me an' dem children."

"You goin' to leave dem wid me though?"

"Yes, Mama."

"An' Donna. Mi have to ask you dis…"

"Yes, Ma'am?"

"Why you don't go an' get a HIV test?"

"Mi well want to do it. But I have to keep strong for mi

children. Suppose mi go take it an' find say mi positive?" Her voice began to break. "Mi not so sure say mi coulda handle dat."

"Hush...hush!" Judith consoled.

In the days that followed, Donna worked on changing her appearance. She cut her hair short, applied too much makeup and altered her clothes. On the morning she left, the parting was painful. Long after she had gone, Judith sat wondering if she would have to raise her grandchildren alone. Would it be a matter of time before their mother would die too? She cursed the cruel fate that had led her child down a path filled with so much pain and uncertainty.

Donna arrived in the little country town of Merchant on the evening of the day she left her mother's house. She easily located the home of her grand aunt, Alice. The old woman lived alone and was very happy to have her. She was a bit surprised at Donna's change in appearance, but she was not about to make her uncomfortable by making any reference to it. Things were already bad enough for the poor girl, Alice reasoned. She had heard of Derrick's death and was ready to accept the story that Donna simply wanted a change of scene.

With her grand-aunt's help, Donna quickly found a small, inexpensive place from which to work. For the first few days she was very nervous, but her ability to work beautifully soon brought her a steady stream of customers. By the end of the first month, she was able to send some money home. Each time they spoke on the phone, Judith would encourage her daughter to get tested.

Three months passed. Life with Aunt Alice was quiet and pleasant. Donna was beginning to get more customers than she could handle. For hours she forgot to worry about anybody from Glandon turning up to blow her cover. She felt great and confident. Happiness seemed accessible again. Then Jean walked into the shop one evening.

Donna nearly fainted. Their eyes met and Jean sat down. For a crazy moment Donna wondered if anybody could hear the bells going off in her head. Why wouldn't this woman leave her alone? To her own surprise, she was able to satisfactorily complete the job she had been doing.

As the customer got up to leave, Jean took her place in the chair. Calmly, she told Donna what she wanted done. Donna was dumbfounded. Jean had lost some weight, but Donna was sure it was the same person. Apprehensively, she worked but as the time elapsed she became a little more relaxed. She felt sure that Jean had not recognized her. As she added the finishing touches, Donna congratulated herself on the effectiveness of her disguise.

She smiled at Jean when the job was done and the woman said, "Thank you, Donna."

Donna was taken aback. "You recognize mi?"

"Of course."

"So what you want from mi now?" Donna asked angrily.

"I got what I wanted. This beautiful hair style," Jean said, patting her head.

"But I don't understand you," Donna said. Her voice was loud and aggressive. "Di last time I see you, you insult mi say mi have AIDS. So is what happen now? Why you change?"

"It's a long story."

"I have time," Donna replied.

Donna sat down and indicated that Jean could sit also if she chose to. They were alone in the place now. Jean took a seat and began her story.

"You know that I knew Derrick, right?"

"I kinda figure dat out," Donna told her.

"Did you know how well I knew him?"

"What you mean?"

"Derrick and I were much more than friends. Donna, we were lovers."

"What!"

"To cut a long story short, "Jean continued, "I just discovered that I am HIV positive."

The words were quietly spoken, but to Donna they were like cruel, hurtful noise that held only the promise of sadness, suffering and pain. She was stunned. She didn't know what to think or say. Jean was pretty, educated and seemed quite well off for a woman her age. So it was difficult to comprehend why she would feel the need to get attached to somebody else's husband. And now she had the virus too. Donna groped for the right words to say.

"Is Derrick you catch it from?" she asked.

"I don't think so." Jean was not offended but neither was she about to apologize. "I love men," she continued. "Real estate is my job, so I always have them around in every place I go. I guess I just wasn't careful enough."

Donna said she was sorry.

"I am sorry, too," Jean said. "But I have lots more life to live. You see how I look good!" she said, twirling around before the mirror playfully.

Donna smiled, thinking for the first time that Jean was really a nice person.

"So you taking your ARV's?" Jean asked.

"What?"

"Your HIV medications."

"Oh…yes," Donna lied.

"Good. I even walk with mine," Jean said, patting her handbag. "This virus is nothing to be ashamed of, my dear," she added. "It is just an illness like diabetes or heart trouble. You'd be surprised at how many people in Glandon just discovered that they have it."

Jean and Donna talked of this and that, and by the end of the day, each knew she had found a new friend.

"You goin' call mi?" Donna asked as she followed Jean to the door.

"Of course!" Jean assured her. "You and I need each other."

"Safe travel," Donna said, smiling. And that was the day she finally decided to get tested. She also vowed to take her medications. She would fight HIV to the end. She would continue to provide for her children. She would die with her dignity intact.

Judith was scolding the children about messing up her immaculately kept house, but they were all beside themselves with excitement when they saw Donna. She giggled when she saw their faces. It was good to be home!

"So is what sweet you?" Judith asked her.

"Nutten. Mi soon help you tidy up."

"Don't worry bout dat ," Judith said, seating herself beside her daughter. "Mi proud a you, Donna."

"T'anks."

"You talk to Aunt Alice?"

"Yes. She say she miss mi. Me miss her too," said Donna.

"So you goin' back to Merchant?"

"Only to look for Aunt Alice," Donna replied. "I plan to do what I tell you say Jean an' me was talkin' about."

Jean was the owner of a small business place in Glandon. She had offered to let Donna use it if she was interested in doing beauty care in the town again. Donna had accepted.

"You tell Jean 'bout you HIV status?" Judith asked.

"Yes," Donna said. "An' I could hardly believe how she happy fo' mi!"

"Is a nice person," Judith said.

"Yes," Donna said. "I believe she woulda feel funny and kinda different like how she have it an'…"

Judith nodded and touched her daughter gently on the shoulder.

"Mi really proud o' you," said Judith. "Mi know you strong. Mi know yuh coulda handle a positive result… But mi glad say you negative."

"Me too, Mama. Me too."

FREDA'S HARVEST

It was a pleasant Tuesday morning. A smell of freshness swirled in the air as droplets of dew yielded to the yellow rays slowly glazing the tops of the magnificent mountains. Even the fog felt good. Freda Martin inhaled the clean country air and thought, as she had often done before, that people who boasted about being born "under the clock" were truly to be pitied. They didn't know what they were missing out here in the country.

Freda moved with the effortless finesse of a jaguar. The huge basket of vegetables on her head seemed simply an extension of her body. Only now and again did a pebble move. Freda had been treading this path for close to forty years, and she had known these pebbles when they were big stones. She was a young woman then, around the time she met and married Samuel Martin.

Unlike Freda, Sam was not from the district of Lushvale. When they met, he had come for a brief visit with his uncle who lived in the community. They met, fell in love and were married in a matter of months. Together, they worked the land Sam had leased from a landowner in the village.

It was hard, back-breaking work, but eventually they would be able to buy the land. Years passed and Freda was about to give up hope of ever having children, when Clive came into their lives.

Sam's joy was boundless. He accepted and treated his son like a gift no man before him had ever had the good fortune to receive. He had great plans for his boy, but the only way he could realize them was through money. The only way Sam knew to make money was by working the land. So when everybody finished working for the day, Sam would continue by the light of a bottle torch.

Freda warned him to take it easy. She told him he wasn't getting any younger. But Sam would not stop.

Clive had been quite young when his tendency to avoid work became apparent.

"Why you don't take Clive to bush sometime?" Freda asked Sam one morning.

"You want me to stop him from school to go to bush?" Sam asked.

"No. But tomorrow is Saturday. Him can come wid you tomorrow."

"You don't see dat Clive don't like bush work?" Sam asked.

"Clive don't seem to like any work at all," replied Freda. "All him like is money!"

"Don't say dat, Freda!"

"You spoilin' him, Sam. Him soon begin to feel like him betta dan you."

"No sah! Him jus' don't cut out fi dis kinda work. An' you know say I want betta tings for him."

"What could be betta dan plantin' food?" Freda asked. "Everybody mus' eat."

Sam walked away, as he usually did when Freda was winning an argument.

Clive had as little interest in school work as he did in farming. When Sam asked the boy's teacher about his school work, Mr. Bryce didn't have the heart to tell him that Clive was the laziest boy in his class. So while Clive's peers qualified for high school through hard work, Clive rode in on the back of the money his father had dug from the jaws of the earth. He did so poorly on his final exams that his father realized he had to shelve his dreams of seeing his son become a lawyer.

Since he seemed to have an affinity for figures, Sam got him into a commercial school in Kingston. True to form, Clive dropped out after a few weeks. He turned up with his suitcase, complaining to his parents about the poor quality of the tuition. Sam took a day off from work and went to check out another school.

Freda was dead set against the idea. She saw what Sam refused to see: Clive was a lazy, selfish boy who cared only about himself. But Sam was a stubborn man and wanted success for his son. The new school fees were higher so Sam worked harder.

Clive was nineteen when his father died in his field of a heart attack. Freda held him partly responsible for what happened to Sam, but she was determined not to show it. She would continue to help this son of hers, even if she was doing so only in his father's memory.

"When you plan to go back to school?" Freda asked him after the funeral.

"I don't plan to go back," said Clive.

"What! Is what you sayin' to mi now, Clive?"

"Well, Mum, is time I try to help out now."

Freda couldn't believe her ears. Was Clive finally beginning to grow a conscience?

"What you mean?" she asked.

"Somebody was telling mi bout a job in Church Town." (Church Town was the nearest town to Lushvale).

"Job?" Freda asked. "But you don't finish school yet."

"Not quite. But I learn all dere is to learn at dat school."

"You comin' wid dat foolishness again?"

"Is not foolishness, Mum. Listen to me. I can work now; I can help you pay fi dis lan'."

"No, no!" Freda disagreed. "You listen to me, Clive. All him life you father did want little more dan fo' you to get a good education. You goin' back to school. You hear mi, Clive? You goin' back to finish up an' graduate!"

"Take it easy, Mum," Clive cautioned. "You goin' to meck everybody hear wi business?"

"I don't care who want to hear!"

"Mum, sit down. I have somethin' to tell you."

"I don't want to hear one ting excep' when you goin' back to school. Jus' go get you tings ready 'cause I want you to leave here by…"

"Mum, I can't go back. Even if I did want to."

Then the story came out: Clive had been expelled from school some weeks ago. When Freda asked why, he gave her a litany of excuses, ranging from his teachers being too hard on him to his fellow students' inability to understand him. He had been hanging out in Church Town, too ashamed to come home, when he got the news of his father's death.

Freda was quiet when Clive finished talking. She wondered if, in some mysterious way, the news of Clive's dismissal from school had been communicated to Sam. Maybe he had finally been forced to accept that his dreams for his son would never be fulfilled. Sam, Freda was thinking, might have died not of a heart attack as the doctor had said, but of a broken heart.

Unable to do otherwise, she went along with the idea and Clive went to work. For three weeks. Then he got sacked. Freda nagged him constantly about his laziness, and Clive fell into a pattern of getting and losing jobs. For peace of mind, Freda felt compelled to accept this situation. She never saw a cent of the money her son made.

Sam was dead, Clive was useless and Freda had to find a way to pay for the land. And so she planned her first work day. Her next door neighbour was the first to arrive.

"Mornin', Miss Freda," Tom said.

"Mornin', Maas Tom. How you do?"

"Me a'right. See a piece a yam here." He handed her three pounds of negro yam.

"Thanks," Freda said as she took it. "Sally comin'?"

"You well know how my wife love cookin'," Tom laughed. "Of course she comin! An' it look to me like is everybody comin' to help you today."

Freda wiped away a grateful tear as she watched Tom walk off into the field carrying his machete. By the middle of the morning, about half of the farmers in Lushvale were present and working hard.

It was a wonderful day. The crackling of the fire-wood flames, the happy chatter of women cooking and men singing as they worked was such an overpowering display of sincere goodness that if the Devil had been passing through that day, even he might have stopped and smiled. Nobody seemed to remember Clive, who slept the day away.

On his twenty-fourth birthday, Clive hosted a bashment party. Freda hated the music so she left the house to spend the evening with Sally. She got back at some minutes to eleven o'clock. The party was over but Clive had a guest. This was not the first time he had brought Blossom to the house, but they both knew that Freda did not like the girl being there so late. Freda went to bed. She woke up in the small hours of the morning to the sound of feminine laughter and went to investigate. Blossom was still in the house. Freda was outraged and she made this clear.

But Clive did not take kindly to what his mother said. He told her that he was a big man now and was perfectly within his rights to invite his girlfriend to spend the night if he wanted to. In fact, he told her, Blossom would be spending many more nights there. He was his father's son, he informed Freda and, as such, he was fully entitled to living with whomever he wanted to in the house his father had built. Freda swore it was the booze talking so she went back to bed. Before she left for the field that morning, she made it clear that she did not want to find the woman there when she returned.

But Blossom was still there and had a suitcase too. Freda didn't do much more talking, and for the first time in his life, Clive saw just how strong his mother was. Firmly and without ceremony, Freda flung him, his belongings, and his Blossom out of her house.

In the years that followed, Freda often wondered if that was the night on which Petal Martin was conceived. If so, she thought, it was not such a bad thing for her to have put up with Clive's slackness that night. For Petal was a fine, fine child. The joy of her heart. Sam would have loved her. Just as everyone in Lushvale did.

Freda met her granddaughter when the child was less than two weeks old. It was October and the field was ripe. Ripe yet green. Freda's heart skipped a beat as she viewed her plantation - cabbage, banana, callaloo and gungo peas. At that moment, Freda was convinced that God's favourite colour was green.

It was another work day, and Freda was up earlier than usual. She was coming down the steps holding her biggest pot, when she heard what sounded like a cat. She ignored it at first, but as the sound continued, she decided to investigate.

Freda approached the direction from which the sound was coming, thinking it was caused by a cat. This puss was just too bright, Freda thought. It deserved a good lick! With stick in hand, she crept stealthily closer. She didn't know when the stick fell from her hand. There before her on the ground was not a cat but a baby.

"Sally!" Freda called out. "Sally, come here quick!"

Freda picked up the child, still shouting for Sally, who came rushing. She was complaining that Freda had woken her up too early. Then she saw the baby.

"Lawd, Freda, is what dat?"

"Is not a 'what' is a 'who'," replied Freda. "Mi jus' find it outside. You know is who it belong to?"

Sally peered at the child.

"No," she replied. "A wha dis now!"

"A inna bush mi find it," Freda said. "Wi have to find di madda."

"You keep sayin, 'it'. Is a boy or girl?"

"Girl," Freda replied.

"But is who coulda wicked enough to do a ting like dis?" Sally asked.

Both were puzzled.

"You know anybody inna Lushvale who pregnant or jus' have baby?" Freda enquired.

"No....Yes!" Sally was thinking hard. She asked Freda, "You rememba dat girl who was friendly wid Clive?"

"Who, Blossom?"

"Yes, Blossom."

"Is what you tryin' to say now, Sally?"

"I not sayin' anyting. But it look funny how as dat girl time come to have baby, you find a baby almost inna your yard."

"But you don't know if she have baby yet," Freda countered.

"I soon find out," Sally said, getting up. Then, as an after thought, she said, "But you don't easy at all eh, Freda. When everybody else a reap food, you a reap baby!"

"You gwaan!" Freda told her. "Jus' hurry up an' go find out is whose baby, meck I set police pon har."

"Yes, Granma!" Sally said, chuckling.

What she found out was that Blossom had given birth a few days ago and had been seen boarding the five o'clock bus out of Lushvale. She did not have a baby with her.

If Freda had any doubts about the paternity of the child, those were allayed in a few short months. Petal's resemblance to her father was uncanny. She was the spitting image of Clive. But that was where the similarities ended. Unlike her father, she was a thoughtful child with a sunny disposition and an aching thirst for knowledge.

When Petal was seven years old, Freda finished paying off for the land. Almost immediately, she started saving for Petal's education. It was the child's dream to become a lawyer, and Freda was determined to succeed where Sam had failed with Clive.

As she got closer to the town, her excitement grew. The sun was getting warmer as the day was fully born. The tiny beads of sweat on Freda's face quickly turned into narrow streams, which gradually meandered their way over places unknown to any man but Samuel Martin. Soon, she would be one with the hustle and bustle of the marketplace. Tuesday was not a regular market day for her, but she had a special reason for being there today.

Clive was to face the court in Church Town that day. He had moved to that town after Freda had thrown him out. Clive had held a job there for quite some time and had even started evening classes. Freda was very pleased when she heard and told herself that she should have kicked him out a long time ago. But old habits die hard, and before long he had resumed his style of wasting time between several different jobs.

Clive, who was now the father of four, had been locked up for assaulting one of his baby-mothers because she had 'shamed' him about maintenance for their child. Freda was not exactly thrilled to break into her little savings to help out. Petal could be entering high school soon, and she would have to finance that all on her own. But Freda was all Clive had, and Sam would have wanted her to help.

She got to the market long before Sally, who was coming by bus. It was almost twelve o'clock, when she left what still remained to be sold, with her friend and neighbour and headed for the court house.

She was beginning to get impatient when Clive was finally brought before the judge. He was a sorry sight. All the resentment Freda had been nursing was replaced by pity and a touch of guilt. He faced the judge, who read the charge like he was either drunk, bored or both.

"How do you plead?" the judge asked.

"Guilty, Your Honour," Clive replied. "But wid explanation."

"Fifteen thousand dollars or six months hard labour," the judge said.

"But..."

The judge cut short Clive's explanation and yelled, "Next case!"

Freda watched as the officers led Clive away. She made her way out and around to the holding area behind the court house, where she asked the officer's permission to speak to her son.

"Clive?" she said, speaking through the opening in the holding area.

He heard and looked at her. His face hardened. "You jus' come?" he asked.

"You didn't see me in di court house?"

"Yes," Clive admitted belligerently. "You have di money?"

"I have mos' a it," Freda said, reaching into her bosom.

"Mos' a it! Mos' a it, Mum?... How mos' a it goin' help mi?"

"Listen to mi, Clive," Freda said. "I have thirteen thousand here. Sally sellin' some food fi mi a market. I goin' go round dere back now. She must sell off by now and can give me two more fi meck up dis."

"An' suppose you don't get di res'?" Clive asked.

"Don't worry youself, man. If di food don't sell, I wi' get di money fi borrow. You not goin' to prison."

"I don't know 'bout dat," Clive replied doubtfully. "Is two night I spen' a jail, an' it wasn't pretty! I sure say prison woulda kill mi."

"But mi tell you not to worry," Freda said. "Time goin' so I have to go look di res' a money now. I soon come," she said, turning to leave.

"Mum," Clive said. Freda turned to look at him. "Why you don't give di officer di money you have now. I can keep it till you come back."

"Why?"

"No special reason," Clive muttered. "I jus' want hold it till you come."

"It look like you don't trus' mi, Clive. A'right I wi' give him."

Freda gave the officer the money, explained the situation to him and asked him to give it to Clive. He looked at his watch and told her to hurry since the prisoner would be taken back to jail shortly if the fine was not paid.

Freda hurried back to the market. Everything had been sold, but she had to go in search of Sally, who had taken the other route to meet her at the court house. When they found each other, Sally gave her the additional money, which was more than what was needed. Clive would be so happy to be free again. She was hurrying back to the court house when she literally ran into Blossom.

Freda reached out to steady the young woman and their eyes met. It had been almost ten years, but it was definitely her. Both were speechless.

"Hi, Miss Freda."

"Hi," Freda replied lamely. She could think of nothing else to say.

"How is Petal?" Blossom asked.

"Who tell you her name?" Freda asked.

Blossom looked away. "Clive," she said. "I hear him was in jail so mi come to see what happenin'."

"You live in dis area again?"

"No, Miss Freda. I live in St. Ann now, but you know how news can travel."

Freda had a million questions to ask her. Like whether or not she had ever seen or was even curious to see her daughter. Like how could she have been sure that the new-born would have been found alive. What had she been doing with her life for the past ten years? Did she have other children?

"You an' Clive is frien' again?" Freda asked.

"No, Ma'am!" Blossom said, staring at the ground. She waited but Blossom seemed to have nothing more to say. Freda suddenly remembered her mission and that she was wasting valuable time.

"I have to go back roun' a court house so I can't stop now," she said abruptly.

She hurried away without another word. As she approached the square, Freda saw that a crowd had gathered. Briefly, she wondered what it was all about. She tried to force her way through, but the crowd was thick.

"Is what happen?" she asked somebody.

"Police shoot a prisoner who did a try escape when dem a carry him 'way."

"But is why people fool so, eh?" Freda asked. "How him expec' fi get way wid so much police out?"

"Somebody say him was tryin' fi get way wid him madda money," the stranger explained. "Commit crime an' 'fraid fi prison! "

Freda stood very still. It couldn't be. She pushed and elbowed her way frantically through the crowd. Then she saw him. Clive was lying on the ground. He seemed peacefully asleep. Only the pool of blood on the ground by his left ear proved that this was to be a permanent sleep for Clive Martin.

Freda crouched beside his body and cradled his head in her lap. She wasn't even aware that she was screaming uncontrollably. Nothing seemed real. The officers stood quietly by as she called down cruel maledictions from heaven upon them. It was a sight that the onlookers would not forget for a long time.

Much later, Sally and Blossom were finally able to coax her to leave the scene.

Clive got a beautiful funeral. Freda received all the support she needed. Yet this did little to lessen the enormous sense of guilt she was experiencing. How had she and Sam failed Clive? What should they have done differently? Was his failure Clive's own fault or theirs? She knew that these questions would never be answered and that dwelling on such thoughts could only destroy her. She had to live for Petal now. She consoled herself with the thought that as Clive's parents they had done their best.

Freda was barely aware that Blossom had followed her home on the evening of Clive's death. Though she was still wary of her, she had to admit that Blossom's help had been invaluable, especially in the time leading up to the funeral. When she heard her story, Freda invited her to stay and continue to help out if she wanted to. Petal and Blossom quickly bonded.

Blossom's grandmother had told her to leave her house as soon as the baby was born. (Her mother had died in childbirth.) On hearing that Clive was involved with another woman in Church Town, she had decided to leave the baby with Freda. She put the child where she knew that Freda would find it.

Blossom had taken the bus bound for the city early that morning, but she had been so sick with worry about her baby that she got off the bus before the journey was over. She was afraid to come back to Lushvale, knowing what she had done. Depressed and confused, she ended up on the street. An older man saw and took pity on her. They eventually got married but had no children.

She had kept in constant touch with Clive, and he had kept her informed on what was happening with Petal. She had even dared to pass by the Lushvale School a few times just to see what her daughter looked like. Clive had given her a picture of the child, and Petal confirmed that she had seen Blossom at least once before.

Blossom's husband eventually became suspicious of her relationship with Clive. The marriage disintegrated, and he ended up filing for divorce. She had recently moved out of the matrimonial home and was looking for work close to Church Town, when she had heard that Clive was in jail.

⚘

About three weeks later, Freda found herself on another stony path. This was the road leading to the teacher's cottage. Mr. Bryce was now the principal at Clive's old school, where Petal was presently a student. He met her as she entered the compound.

"Mrs. Martin!" he called out. "I was just coming to see you. Well, well! Great minds do think alike. Come this way. Come in and have a seat."

He led her onto the verandah of the house and put out a chair for her. Freda wondered why he was in such a jubilant mood. He was at Clive's funeral, so he should be aware that she was still in mourning. She was beginning to find his gleeful attitude offensive.

"I have great news for you," said Mr. Bryce.

"What?"

"Petal passed with flying colours! "

Freda began to cry.

"I know you just buried Clive," he said, "but life goes on, Mrs. Martin. This is good news."

Freda tried to wipe away her tears.

"Is dat mi come to talk to you 'bout, sir," Freda said.

"I don't understand."

"Petal can still spend another year in primary school, right?"

"Yes. But…"

"All what I did save fi Petal education get use up in buryin' Clive," said Freda. "She can't go to high school now. So I come to ask you to keep her for one more year so I can get a chance to work an' save again."

Mr. Bryce grinned broadly.

"Is what, Mr. Bryce?" Freda asked. "You don't hear what mi say?"

"You have nothing to worry about," he told her. "Petal got a government scholarship!"

"Government scholarship?"

"Yes. All her expenses will be taken care of by the government. Her high school education will totally be their responsibility."

"I…I don't know how to t'ank you, Teacher."

"No, Mrs. Martin," Mr. Bryce said. "It is we who must thank you. Petal has put our school on the map!" He could hardly contain his excitement. Then he put his hand on Freda's shoulder. "And you did it all alone. You are a strong woman, Freda Martin, and you have reaped what you sowed. Petal has done us proud, and the best is yet to come."

SUGAR FOSTER

If niceness was money, Sugar would have been rotten rich. He wasn't bad looking. He was tall and dark, had soft hair and eyes to die for. His eye lashes may have been too curly for a man, and his nose could have been a little smaller. Had he been of high society, the women of his sphere would have described him as "rather elegant" when he dressed for special occasions. But his laugh was his most distinctive feature.

When Sugar laughed it was like a shy, mischievous drum roll was started in his belly by a pair of childlike hands. By the time it got to his windpipe, an orchestra of horns, cymbals and flutes had taken over. And when that sound would hit the air, the resonance of its melody would shake and shatter. But it was his love for sugar cane that gave him his nickname.

It wasn't that Sugar had much to laugh about. After the death of his father when he was just five, Agnes Foster raised Sugar by herself. She was a sickly woman who could hardly afford to send the child to school. As a young man, Sugar farmed the small plot of land his father had bought and worked in the cane fields during crop season. When Miss Agnes died, he became the owner of the little house he had known all his life.

Like Sugar, Julie Maxwell was an only child. Both were born and grew up in Burn Meadow at a time when sugar was still king. And like Sugar, she knew well the community's vast cane fields, parched grasses and empty days. Julie was a slender, attractive, quick-witted girl who had inherited her mother's sense of style. Miss Beatrice, the biggest dressmaker in Burn Meadow, was a single mother. She had big dreams for her daughter and regarded Julie's being in love with Sugar Foster as the girl's biggest drawback. Miss Beatrice hated Sugar's poverty. So when Vincent Harris, a local businessman, began to show interest in Julie, Miss Beatrice was excited.

"Him like you!" she told the girl.

"How you know dat, Mum?"

"You don't see how him look pon you?"

"But him plenty older dan me," Julie objected. "An' I hear him have plenty bad ways too."

"So what?" Miss Beatrice retorted. "You know anybody who have so-so good ways?"

Julie had no response.

"Listen," Miss Beatrice continued. "I know you want to go college, but tings not so pretty right now. Mos' people buyin' ready-made clothes nowadays. Why you don't tek di job Vincent offerin' you, so you can save toward you education?"

So Julie went to work as a cashier at Harris' Dry Goods Store. Vincent was not famous for his good deeds. He was a stodgily built, brown-skinned man with hair almost completely grey, belying the fact that he was still on the better side of fifty. He had a small, round face that emphasized his humongous ears. Julie still saw Sugar every weekend but ended up spending more time with her boss.

Despite his spotty reputation, Vincent was kind and respectful toward Julie and, in time, she became more tolerant of him. She began to see Sugar less frequently, and Sugar comforted himself with the thought that his girl was just busy with work. But when he heard of her engagement to Vincent, he was devastated. Miss Beatrice was elated.

"Lawd, a can't believe it," she gushed. "Mi daughta gettin' married to a money man! What a something?"

Julie watched her with much less enthusiasm.

"You goin' wear the bes' weddin' dress anybody inna Meadow evva see!" Beatrice declared. Then, calmly, she asked, "You tell Sugar yet?"

Julie hung her head.

"No," she muttered. "But him mus' hear like everybody else…Poor Sugar!"

"Poor Sugar, what?" Miss Beatrice shot back. "Nuh worry wid dat, mi dear! Everybody haffi look out fi demself."

⚶

Sugar eventually managed to accept the fact that Julie was to be another man's wife, but he wanted to say his last goodbyes and give her something he had had made specially for her. But his messages asking her for a last meeting with him went unanswered. Sugar needed closure and the strength to move on with his own life.

Late one Thursday morning, he donned his best clothes and climbed the hill to the store where Julie worked. (Everybody in Burn Meadow knew that Vincent went into town every Thursday to buy goods.) From behind her counter, Julie saw Sugar walk in and she froze. He smiled and her knees went weak. This was the reason she had ignored his messages to meet with her.

"Hi, Julie," Sugar grinned.

"Hi," Julie muttered.

"You lookin' good."

"Thanks."

Neither of them seemed to know what next to say.

"A bring something fo' you," Sugar said, handing her a little package.

Without a word, she took it and began to remove the wrapping. Neither of them was aware that Vincent, whose vehicle had broken down, was quietly watching them from the back of the store, a beer in his hand.

When Julie saw Sugar's gift, her mouth fell open. It was a beautiful silver brooch in the shape of an L, studded with tiny diamonds that winked in the light.

But you can't afford dis! Julie thought to herself.

"You like it?" Sugar asked.

Julie nodded.

"Someting new to wear to you weddin'."

Julie bit her lips and tried to wipe the tears away. It was at that precise moment that Vincent sneaked up behind Sugar.

"What a way you bright!" he yelled.

Sugar turned, startled, to face him.

"Vincent!" Julie shouted.

"A wha you believe, you have wha Julie want?" Vincent continued. "A trouble you a look?"

"No," Sugar started to say. "I jus' bring a little present fi…"

Before he could finish his answer, Vincent took a step forward and emptied the contents of the bottle in his hand into Sugar's face.

"Tek dat, you dog you!" he said with venom. "A mus' dat you come yah fah!"

Sugar cursed some bold words. Instinctively, his hands went to his face as he tried desperately to prevent the liquid from blocking his vision. By this time, Julie had left the counter and was now in front with the two men. She placed herself between them and turned to Vincent.

"You mad?" she demanded. "Look wha you do to Sugar?"

Vincent ignored her. "Lef' mi woman!" he yelled at Sugar.

"Stop you nonsense, Vincent," Julie said hotly. "You jus' makin a ass o' youself!"

"Gimme dat likkle foolishness him say him bring fi you," Vincent said, reaching for the brooch in Julie's hand. "Meck I fling it…"

He never finished the sentence as, with her other hand, Julie struck a blow to his face that would probably have floored a weaker man. Sugar watched in silent amazement. Hurriedly, Vincent backed away, fingering the side of his face, which had begun to turn pink. Cautiously, he watched Julie. Then he looked at Sugar.

"You see wha you cause now!" he whined.

"Sugar don't cause nutten!" Julie bellowed. "You is di cause a all a dis! Wha you fling beer inna him face fo', Vincent? Suppose him did decide fi beat you up?"

By this time, Sugar had managed to get much of the beer off himself and was watching the situation with guarded amusement.

"Is me him come to," Julie shouted, "Not you. Dis is none a your business! I have a good mind call police pon you!"

"'Police'?" Vincent echoed. "But what is dis!...Police?"

"Yes, police!" Julie reaffirmed. "Wha you assault Sugar fo'?"

"Look here, Julie," Vincent said after a while. "I don't like how you goin' on, you know. No, man. Don't like it at all! Is me you want or Sugar?"

Julie looked at him. Then she turned and looked long at Sugar. A long silence followed, heaving and simmering with the pregnancy of two possibilities. The two seemed unaware only of each other; totally unconscious of Vincent and his increasing discomfiture.

"Meck up you mine!" Vincent yelled.

Slowly, deliberately, Julie removed her engagement ring.

"Sugar," she said, handing the ring back to Vincent.

꙳

Miss Beatrice was stunned at the turn of events. She told Julie how hard she was finding it to accept the fact that she had actually given birth to such an ungrateful and stupid child. Over and over she said it. When Julie could no longer take it, she left and moved in with Sugar. Less than a month later, they were married by a J.P. in Kingston.

"She goin' to regret it," Miss Beatrice told Vincent.

Vincent nodded in agreement. Their mutual disappointment had drawn them closer.

"But it not goin' go so!" he said ominously.

"Wha you goin' do?' Miss Beatrice asked.

"You wi see!" Vincent said.

"Don't try hurt mi daughta you know, Vincent!"

"No, Miss B," Vincent assured her. "Julie still goin' to be my wife. But Sugar...Well, everybody goin' see!"

Before the end of his first year of marriage to Julie, Sugar became father to a baby girl. Over the course of the next three years, Julie gave birth to a son and another daughter. Sugar continued to work the land after finishing work in the cane fields, and Julie raised a few chickens. But times were hard for them.

Sugar soon found that he had enough money to buy a cow. He called the cow Eve. Every year after that, Eve produced a strong, robust calf and her calves were as fertile as herself. Before long, Sugar became the owner of quite a decent herd of cattle. Things were beginning to look up.

Miss Beatrice watched everything from a distance. Though she doted on her grandchildren, she was very cold toward her daughter and Sugar.

"Look like tings a improve fi Julie and her husban'," she told Vincent one evening.

"Sugar a still small fry!" Vincent said viciously.

Miss Beatrice cleared her throat.

"Well accordin' to what you did say afta dem married, I did tink Sugar woulda dead or cripple long time!"

"Mi have sometin' fi tell you," Vincent said.

"Wha dat?"

"You ever hear 'bout dat workman who live top a one high hill inna St. Thomas?"

"Mi hear 'bout him," Miss Beatrice confessed. "Hear say him work expensive."

"Same one!" Vincent said. "Is him I did go to 'bout Sugar, likkle afta him married Julie."

"Wha! So how nutten nevva happen?' Miss Beatrice asked. "Not dat mi hate Sugar, you know. Him not really a bad person. Is jus dat mi nevva want him fi married to..."

"Hear mi!" Vincent cut in. "Di man say Sugar a work wid a higha spirit!"

Miss Beatrice was amazed.

"Higha spirit?" Miss Beatrice asked. "Wha dat mean?"

"Mean say di man couldn't touch him, cause Sugar obeah more powerful," Vincent explained.

"What is dis!" Miss Beatrice was beyond surprise. "Higha spirit," she kept repeating. "But hol' on, Vincent," she then added. "Which part Sugar did fi get money fi pay fi dat kine a obeah? Noh jus' recently him start do likkle betta?"

"I don't know," Vincent said, irritated. "Maybe him a work di obeah himself."

He left shortly after, and Miss Beatrice sat wondering over what he had said. In a place like Burn Meadow, where the power of black magic was both feared and revered, Sugar Foster was the only person she knew who dared to laugh at obeah. Nobody had, as yet, managed to convince him that anything supernatural could affect him for good or evil. Not even something as basic as a ring or a charm would the man wear to protect himself.

Miss Beatrice was deeply puzzled. What if that higher spirit was something good? Something pure and different which had nothing to do with obeah? She knew Sugar. It was possible. Maybe even likely. For hours she thought about it. Then she came to the conclusion that it was time for her to stop being angry with Julie and her husband. She could maybe even offer to give them a boost financially. If Sugar wouldn't be too proud to accept it.

He was at first, but Julie convinced him to take the money as a loan. Sugar used it to lease a piece of land, which he used to plant his own cane fields. Then he began to expand and renovate their little house. Things were definitely improving. People who had had a problem with Julie's initial rejection of Vincent, now decided that she was perfectly right to have hooked up with Sugar.

Sugar was generous. The more he got, the more he gave away. Most of the children in Burn Meadow who had no daddy called him "Daddy Sugar," since it was he who gave them lunch money and bought them school books. Widows and orphans turned to him and none went away empty-handed. When men began migrating to England, Sugar helped pay their plane fare. He even put suits on the backs of some of those who left.

Now that Sugar was prospering, Vincent was beginning to get very uncomfortable. People were looking at him funny. No longer would anybody seek him out to tell him "How-di-do". He had to greet them first and many would reply, "Yes, Vincent!" or "Oh deh, Vin!". Not "Mr. Vincent" or "Mr. Harris" as they used to say. One or two had even had the temerity to snigger at his back. This was simply not good.

Mr. Harris decided to seek the services of an obeah man even more powerful and expensive than the one in St. Thomas. But this man only managed to confirm and add to what the other had said: Sugar was an obeah worker himself and his obeah was "bigger, badder and better" than all the local obeah combined.

Vincent came away, fuming. So it was foreign obeah! But how else could Sugar have taken Julie away from him? How else could a little nobody like that have acquired such good fortune in so short a time? Sugar had not played fair, but since he couldn't beat him, he had to join him, but just to find out about this extra special obeah.

✺

Sugar and Julie were relaxing on their front porch one Sunday afternoon, when Vincient turned up.

"Evenin', Mister. Evenin', Missis," he greeted them with a great show of humility.

"Hey, Missa Vincent!" Sugar responded cheerfully. "Long time no see. Come inside, man!"

"T'ank you," Vincent said, taking the seat offered to him. "So everyting a'right?" he asked. "Hope you don't still bex wid mi."

"No, sah!' Sugar replied. "Look how long dat happen?" He looked at his wife. "Right, Julie?"

Julie smiled.

"I don't even rememba' 'bout anyting," she said. "Is a long, long time now."

Vincent nodded, relieved.

"So what bring you here dis evening?" Sugar asked him.

Vincent cleared his throat. "Man talk," he said drily.

"Okay," Julie said, getting up. "Meck I leave you two to unoo man talk."

"Maybe you coulda bring wi some drinks afterward," Sugar suggested as she left.

"A'right."

Julie went into the house.

"So what's on your min' now?" Sugar asked Vincent.

"Well...I don't know if you hear 'bout it, but I not keepin' too well lately, you know."

"No," Sugar said. "What is di nature o' di problem?"

"I don't even know."

"So you don't go to docta?"

"Is dat I want to talk to you 'bout. I need yuh help, Sugar. No local docta can solve my problem."

"You need a foreign docta?"

Vincent cleared his throat again.

"Wi a two big man, right, Sugar?"

"Right."

"So I want you put mi on to your workman."

"Workman?"

"Yes. I hear 'bout di man who a work fi you a foreign." He then gestured toward the lush surroundings. "Who a bring you all dis good luck."

"Wha?" Sugar was surprised. "A obeah you a talk 'bout? But you know say mi nuh inna dat, man."

"You lie!" Vincent said rudely.

"I don't know is who coulda tell you say..." Sugar started to say.

"Done wid dat now!" Vincent interrupted. Then he laughed. "You fool everybody, man," he said. "'Bout you don't believe inna obeah!"

Sugar sat very still. His eyes took on a glazed look as they appeared to stare through Vincent's clean-shaven face into his stubbornly twisted soul. Vincent began to feel uncomfortable.

"So you hear say I have a foreign obeah man?" Sugar asked quietly.

"Yes," Vincent replied. "Jus' help mi out an' tell mi how fi get in touch wid him, man."

"Julie!" Sugar called out. "We not goin' to need any drinks."

Vincent sensed that things would not be turning out as he had hoped. He stood up as he saw Sugar begin to rise from his own chair.

"You know wha kinda docta you need?" Sugar asked him.

"Wha'?"

"Head docta! Di only part o' you wha' sick is you head, Vincent!"

"But..."

"Whoever tell you say I a work obeah know more 'bout my business dan me!" Sugar continued angrily. "Gwan a you yard, man!"

Vincent beat a hasty retreat, calling Sugar a mean and selfish man who would live to regret not sharing his secret with him.

Little more than a week later, things began to change. Several heads of Sugar's cattle were found dead in the pasture. Vincent had paid somebody to poison the water source. The enemy continued to spread money around, and Sugar's cane fields mysteriously caught fire one night. Vincent had started telling people that Sugar was experiencing a change in fortunes because he had not been paying the foreign obeah man who worked for him.

When their youngest child began to be affected by the situation, Julie decided to take her to spend a few days with her grandmother. Vincent was basking in the glow of his victory when he heard this latest development. He assumed that Julie had left Sugar, and he got drunk with success. He decided to finally humiliate and finish him off by running Sugar out of Burn Meadow. Vincent found a young man he knew was unemployed.

"You want some easy money, Radcliff?" he asked him.

Radcliff nodded. "But how?" he asked.

"Jus' by puttin' likkle meat inna Sugar Foster roof."

Radcliff was puzzled. "Why?" he asked.

"You don't haffi worry 'bout dat part, man," Vincent said. "Jus' meck sure you do it late a night so nobody don't see you."

Radcliff was reluctant. He had known Sugar all his life and had always liked and respected him. But he had not had a good meal in days, so he took the money.

"You wi get di balance when di job done," Vincent told him."

The next day vultures surrounded Sugar's house. He was thankful that no other member of his family was home to endure the frightful experience. His two older children were away at boarding school. He prayed and asked God to let him know what he had done wrong so he could make amends and get his life on track again. When the meat dried up the vultures went away.

Vincent went back to Radcliff and told him to get lots more meat this time. But the youngster refused.

"No," he said. Sugar had helped his father years ago when he had wanted to "go a foreign," the young man explained. He should never have done "such a wicked ting" in the first place, and he had no intention of repeating it.

So Vincent decided to take matters into his own hands. Late that night, he went to Sugar's house carrying a bag of raw meat and a ladder. He saw a light and peeped in through a window. Sugar was reading.

"Bet a Bible di idiot a read," Vincent said to himself. "Like Bible can run john crow!"

He had thought the man would have been asleep by now, but he decided to chance it anyway. Vincent was no longer a young man, and his aching joints reminded him of that as he slowly climbed the ladder. Just as he thought he had made it, he lost his balance and fell ignominiously on top of a huge stack of pimento leaves which had been left in the back yard.

Sugar heard the noise and went outside. He found Vincent curled up in a foetal position on the ground. He was moaning but had suffered no serious harm.

"What you doin' here, Vincent?" he asked.

Sugar repeated his question but still got no answer. Then he saw the meat and the ladder and immediately understood. Now he knew that the man moaning at his feet had been the source of all his problems. Not the wrath of God. Not anything supernatural. Nothing he couldn't handle. Just Vincent. A great and wonderful sense of relief washed over him like a warm shower on a chilly night in Mandeville.

Sugar laughed long, hard and happily in the cool, quiet darkness of the spicy September night. The stars seemed to hear him and twinkled brighter than usual.

When he got control of himself, Sugar took hold of Vincent and sat him roughly at the foot of a mango tree in the yard.

"You nuh shame?" he asked. "A big, important man like you lef' you yard come a climb mi house inna di middle night. Jus fi mash up mi life. Wait till I call dung everybody pon you!" Sugar said and headed for the gate.

"Do, Sugar!" Vincent begged. "Mi a beg you nuh do dat, man!"

"But you deserve it," Sugar said. "An' more to!"

"If you do dat, mi goin' haffi lock dung mi place and run way, Sugar!"

Sugar had stopped moving, and Vincent could sense that he had changed his mind.

"If you did tell mi who a you obeah man, none a dis woulda happen!" he murmured sourly.

Sugar walked back over to him and grabbed him by the scuff of his neck.

"Listen to mi, Vincent Harris," he said. "You listenin'?" Then he took hold of Vincent's ears and shouted, "Mi don't have nuh obeah man! I don't work obeah! You understan' now?"

"A'right!" Vincent cried. "Leggo mi ears, man!"

"You sure you believe it?" Sugar asked, clutching Vincent's huge ears even tighter and jerking him around.

"YES!" Vincent yelled.

"You sure you goin' rememba?"

"Yes, yes! You a go pop off mi ears dem?"

Sugar let go and leaned against the mango tree.

"What a man head tough!" he said.

"So how you get through so good?" Vincent asked, slowly stroking his ears.

Sugar was silent for some time.

"I don't even sure. I jus' do as much good as I can, work hard and beg God fi help mi wid di res'."

"No sah!" Vincent objected. "You expec' me fi believe say…"He stopped as Sugar looked menacingly at him. "A'right… If you say so."

"An' look how you mess up mi life, just through foolishness!"

"Don't worry 'bout dat," Vincent said, dragging himself to his feet. "I goin' to meck it up to you "

"How you mean?" Sugar asked.

"Mi owe you cause you coulda run mi outa di place tonight. So I goin' to give you back all dem cow what dead."

"Wha 'bout mi cane?"

"Me wi work pon dat to," Vincent vowed. "An' if dem don't ready by next crop season, I wi' set you up pon a nice little piece a money."

By the pale light of the moon, Sugar watched Vincent, wondering if he would ever live up to what he was saying.

"Wha 'bout dem lie you tell 'bout mi?" he asked.

"Dat easy to fix more dan everyting else," Vincent declared. "Is only Julie mi can't get back fi you," he said with a gleam in his eyes.

"How you mean 'get back'?" Sugar asked. "Julie an' my daughta comin' back home tomorrow."

"Oh…" Vincent could barely hide his disappointment. He had still not accepted that Julie had, without the urgings of obeah, chosen Sugar over him.

"Well, mi a leave now," he said then. "Don't worry youself, Sugar. Everyting soon a'right again. An' nobody but you an' me must know 'bout what happen tonight, right sah?"

"Right," Sugar said. "Mi an' Julie wi keep yuh secret as long as you do what you say you goin' do."

"You can depen' pon dat, man!"

Sugar watched as Vincent hobbled off into the night. He took up the bag of meat and buried it. The ladder remained in the backyard till a passing vagrant took possession of it.

Sugar doubted very much that Vincent would keep his word, but he did. In a few short months, Sugar Foster and his relatives were happy again. It was as if nothing bad had happened.

One Sunday afternoon, Vincent invited himself to dinner at Sugar's house. The children were away but Miss Beatrice was there. They invited him in.

"You finish eat a'ready?" Sugar asked.

"Mi a'right," Vincent replied. "I feel like mi belly soon bus!"

"Before good food waste, meck belly bus!' Miss Beatrice chimed in.

"Don't listen to Mum, you hear," Julie advised. "Wi don't want dis to be you last meal."

"Talkin' 'bout last meal," Vincent said. "Mi hear say dem celebratin' Last Suppa up a church next week. You comin', Beatrice?"

The others looked at him, surprised.

"Mi can't believe wha mi a hear," Miss Beatrice exclaimed. "Vincent Harris a go a church! A when you turn Christian?"

Vincent blushed. "Mi nuh Christian," he said. Then he looked at Sugar. "But somebody convince mi say God really help people so…"

He then seemed to be at a loss for words.

"…So you want to check it out fi youself," Sugar finished for him, then turned to Miss Beatrice. "So go wid him, nuh Miss B?"

"Yes, gwan wid him," Julie urged her mother. "You have plenty church clothes."

"Jus tell mi is what time so mi can pick you up," Vincent suggested.

"Dat soun' like a date to!" Sugar grinned.

"But is wha' unoo a get mi inna, eh?" Miss Beatrice asked, feigning annoyance. "So you an' Sugar not goin', Julie?"

"Me wi go," Julie replied. "Wha 'bout you, Sugar?"

"I wi go if Julie say 'yes' to a question I been askin' her,"

"A wha kine a question dat now?" Vincent muttered.

"Watch you mout', Sugar!" Miss Beatrice warned. "A eat wi a eat."

"I want Julie to agree to go college," Sugar said. "Unoo help mi convince her say she can still go."

"You comin' wid dat again!" said Julie. "Wha dat haffi do wid church?"

"But him right," Vincent affirmed. "Nobody evva too ole to learn. Di olda di moon di brighta it…"

"T'ank you, Missa…"

Julie cut Sugar off. "A call you a call mi ole, Vincent?"

"No, but…"

"But what a feisty…"

"Done!" Miss Beatrice interrupted. "One ting at a time. I know I ole an' soon dead, so I goin' to church wid Vincent… I wi work pon Julie fi you, Sugar. Right now, wi goin' finish eat so di place can tidy up, right?"

"Right," everybody muttered.

They dug into the food again. Julie threw her husband a dirty look. Sugar winked at her and chuckled. The chuckle then turned into a full-blown laugh. Vincient joined in and then Miss Beatrice. Julie did not.

OBEAH AND THE UNBORN

"Mawnin', Miss Rosa!" the little girl called.

"Mawnin', nice girl! You goin' a school?"

"Yes, Ma'am."

"A'right. Run gwan quick before bell ring," Rosa Green advised. "You nuh want teacha beat you dis mawnin', right?"

"Noooo," the child replied, hastening her steps. "Mi fraid a beatin' bad!"

"Mi know," Rosa chuckled.

She watched, amused, as the little girl broke into a run. Rosa liked little children but was partial to the likes of this "pretty hair" one.

Miss Rosalind Green was one of the most important residents in the district of Cattle Ridge. She owned and made her living from the biggest shop in the district. Miss Green had an only son, Karl, whom she loved more than life itself. Nobody in the village had ever seen Karl's father, but they had heard that he was of Irish descent.

Karl was a decent, hard-working young man and was liked by everybody in Cattle Ridge. He seemed completely unaware of any difference between himself and the others whose skin was of a darker hue. He was humble and pleasant. His mother had had ambitions of making him into a white collar worker, but Karl was determined to become a farmer and he refused to be dissuaded.

What this mother still clung to was the dream of one day having a crop of beautiful, fair-skinned grandchildren to call her "Grandma". She had often spoken of this to Karl, whose response was always a chuckle and the advice that his mother should not count her "grand-chickens" before they were hatched.

So when Karl began to show interest in a dark-skinned girl, Miss Green did not hesitate to show her disapproval.

"But is what dat you gone pick up?" she asked him.

"But you well fresh you know, Mama!" Karl responded. "Is who you callin 'what'? Bernice is a very nice young lady. I don't see anyting wrong wid her."

"Karl," his mother tried to reason with him. "You is mi only chile. You don't expect dat I woulda want di bes' fo' you?"

"Yes, Mama, an' I t'ank you. But I still don't see anyting wrong wid Bernice."

"You don't see her colour?" the woman asked.

"Her colour?" Karl turned to face her. "Her colour? What dat have to do wid anyting? Black skin don't mean black heart! You should know dat. Bernice is a kind, decent person."

Miss Green was exasperated.

"Is me you want look shame," she said. "A nice brown skin boy like you should try to hold up you head. Instead you gone get youself mix up wid dis black gal!"

"Is what you talkin' 'bout, Mama? No matter how fair a person skin is, if him not fully white, him black! You nevva know dat?" He smiled patiently at his mother. "You an' Bernice have di same colour," Karl said. "Maybe dat is why you both so nice! You two jus' goin' have to learn to get along."

Rosa's expression did not change. Karl blew her a kiss and took off to his banana field. His mother went to serve a customer and the matter was forgotten for a while.

Some weeks later, her best friend Margaret paid her a visit. They sat close to each other as they examined the latest developments in Cattle Ridge, in the light of the local gossip. Rosa was startled when her friend said, "So you soon turn granny, mi fren."

"What? Is wha' you talkin' 'bout now?" Rosa asked.

"Mi say it look like you soon turn granny pon wi!" Margaret repeated.

"Me? Explain youself, Margaret."

"Is di gal Bernice. It look to me like she pregnant."

"Lawd Jesas!"

"Don't get so frighten, man," Margaret continued. "Mi don't sure say she pregnant. Mi jus' a say how she look fat. Ask Karl 'bout it when him come."

Miss Green cleared her throat nervously.

"Look here, Maggie. You know what....Is a whole heap a tings I have to do before night, you know. Why you don't come back tomorrow?"

Margaret got up to go. "So is why you a run mi out a di place so sudden?" she asked.

"Tomorrow, man. Tomorrow wi talk again," Rosa replied.

"A' right. Mi wi' see you," Margaret said as she left.

His mother could hardly wait for Karl to come home so she could accost him about what she had heard. She heard him come in long after she had locked up the shop. Rosa jumped out of bed and hurried to the confrontation.

"Is where you comin' from dis time o' night?" she shouted.

"Mama?" Karl turned to look at her. "Is what you doin' up so late? You not gettin' any younger, you know!"

But Rosa was hopping mad and in no joking mood.

"Is dat dutty gal what you tek up wid! You is a big man now, but you still livin' unda my roof. I not puttin' up wid dis slackness no more. Shape up or ship out!"

The words were hardly out of her mouth when she began to wish with all her might that she could take them back. The two stared at each other in silence for some seconds.

"Okay, Ma'am. If is so you want it. You know how long I been askin' Bernice to come talk to you? But she know you hate her, so she 'fraid. Wi kinda get a place a'ready, anyway. Good night, Mama," said Karl.

He went to his room and straight to bed. Rosa went back to bed too, but she slept very little that night. That was the last night that Karl slept at his mother's house.

In the days that followed, Karl saw what seemed like a change in his mother's attitude. She begged him to come back home. She seemed sad and lonely, and he felt sorry for her. She was not so quick to criticize his girlfriend, but whenever he tried to talk about her, Rosa grew silent. She couldn't help asking whether or not Bernice was pregnant and was relieved when he told her she wasn't. They had no plans to start a family until they were married, Karl told her.

When he said that, Rosa said to herself, *Family! Wid dat black gal? Over my dead body!*

She could not have selected a more unfortunate set of words.

✽

A few weeks later, Bernice walked shyly into Rosa's shop. She was bubbling with excitement and holding a telegram.

"Mornin', Miss Green."

"Mornin'," Rosa replied crisply.

"I jus' get a telegram fo' Karl."

"Oh?"

"Him get call to do farm work in America. See di telegram here," the girl said, handing it over.

Miss Green stiffly took the telegram and tried to read it, but she was so angry that she could hardly see. Karl had not even told her that he was seeking employment abroad. She felt betrayed. Obviously, the only person he cared about these days was this girl smiling broadly in front of her. But she kept her composure and asked, "So is when him goin'?"

"It in di telegram" Bernice told her. "Next week Friday."

"Oh yes," she said, looking back at the paper. "Next week Friday. Tell Karl to come see mi later," she said as she handed it back.

Miss Green locked the shop early that evening. She was not happy. Rosa was feeling pain, disappointment and white-hot rage. She could not allow somebody like Bernice to take her son away from her. What of the grandchildren?

A few nights later, she was on her way to visit one of Jamaica's most famous obeah men. The car belonged to Old Edwin, who was famous for saying that his car was almost as old as himself. But it was a reliable car, and in less than three hours they had arrived. Obeah was expensive, but she was willing to make the sacrifice.

Edwin took silent note of the fact that the bag his passenger had gone into the yard with was much bulkier when she came back out. She hardly looked at him. What he didn't know was that she was a little afraid. Rosa was remembering how the man had impressed upon her to be careful with the "the parcel". It was deadly. The first person to walk over it, he had said, would be dead in a matter of weeks. It was up to her to make sure that only the intended victim would suffer.

Driver and passenger spoke little on the way back. Edwin was used to minding his own business, and the lady's mind seemed to be very far away. They arrived back in Cattle Ridge in the wee hours of Sunday morning.

During the week of Karl's departure, his mother seemed happy. He naturally assumed that she was happy for him. On the day he left, she did not accompany him to the airport. He was disappointed, but he kissed her goodbye and promised to keep in touch.

They arrived at the Norman Manley Airport in good time. Karl and Bernice were about to say their goodbyes when it was announced that the flight for the farm workers was cancelled. Departure was rescheduled for late the following day. Karl was more than a little annoyed, but Bernice was happy to have him for a few more hours. It was eight o'clock when they set off on the journey back home.

At about that same time, Rosa Green was moving stealthily along the foot-path that led to her son's home. She was carrying the parcel from the do-good man. The moon was big and bright. She crept through the small wooden gate and walked up to the little house. Carefully, she hid the parcel below the entrance to the house. Briefly, she noted that Bernice was doing an excellent job of keeping the steps and surroundings clean. Then she turned and left as quickly and quietly as she had come.

When Karl, Bernice and their friends got back to Cattle Ridge that night, everybody was fast asleep. It was almost midnight when the couple crossed the threshold of the house they called home.

Big Moon was just thinking about making way for his hotter and brighter rival, when he glimpsed Rosa retrieving the parcel. He had watched her place it there earlier. Unlike him, she had no idea that Karl was inside the house. Big Moon watched as she disposed of the despicable object in a deserted pond nearby. He thought to himself that she would not have dared to do such evil when the hot sun of heaven was up and about.

Shop opened early that Saturday morning. Rosa was very excited and a little nervous. She sat gazing down the road. She was sure that Bernice would turn up before long to tell her of Karl's departure.

It was about mid-morning when her eyes fell upon Bernice and Karl walking up the hill towards the shop. For a moment Rosa just stared, hoping that she was watching a spiteful mirage. Her heart stopped briefly as the goods she was weighing fell to the floor. She ran out of the shop shouting: "Karl, Karl! What happen? I tink you gone! What happen, Karl?... What happen? What you doin' here?"

"But I nevva know say you so well want to get rid o' mi!" Karl said, reaching out to her.

Miss Green stamped her foot in agitation and grabbed hold of his arm.

"Dis is no jokin' matter!" she cried. "Tell mi what happen. What you doin' here?" Her lips were trembling as she asked desperately, "You a'right Karl? You a'right?"

Karl held on to his mother to calm her.

"Easy, Mama," he said. "Don't get so excited. Is jus' dat di flight get cancel. I goin' back later. Everyting a'right."

"Come, Miss Green," Bernice said, taking her arm. "Come sit down. If you did come a airport wid wi, you wouldn't get such a bad shock."

Rosa allowed herself to be led into the shop, trying her hardest to keep calm. She couldn't help asking: "Is which one of you did go into di house firs' las' night?"

Karl looked at her with concern in his eyes.

"What dat have to do wid anyting, Mama?" he asked. "You sure you feelin a'right?"

Rosa shook her head as if to clear it and laughed vacantly.

"Is a surprise," was all she could come up with.

"Surprise? Surprise for who?" Bernice asked.

"Both of you," she answered lamely.

"So how you did know say both of us comin' back?" Karl asked.

Rosa tried to laugh again, but it came out hollow.

"Di two a you confusin' mi, man!" she said. "Jus' tell mi which one o' you did go into di house firs' las' night."

The couple watched her gravely.

"If I rememba right, both of us did go in one time," said Bernice.

"Yes. But one mus' go in first'. Which one o' you —"

Karl cut her off at that point.

"Mama," he said. "What is dis all about? Something happen since wi leave?"

Rosa could see that they were both becoming suspicious, so she compelled herself to stop speaking. With as much composure as she could muster, Rosa gave them the goods they had come for. As Bernice took the things, Karl said, "Mama, you don't look too right to me at all, you know. Maybe you gettin' flu. Is either dat or dis travel excitement get to you. You should go lie down now. When I leavin' later, I goin' check you."

"A'right," Miss Green said quietly.

If somebody had asked her to recount the events of the rest of that day, she would not have been able to. She felt dizzy and scared. She vaguely remembered Karl bidding her goodbye as he started on his second trip to the airport. She had to take a sleeping pill that night.

She woke up groggy and weak. The whole morning she waited anxiously for Bernice to come by. Evening came but the girl did not show up, so she sent to call her. Bernice bounced healthily into the shop, her breasts jiggling like jello. Rosa was hoping that some sign of the parcel's effect would have begun to show on the young woman.

⚜

Several weeks passed. Karl kept in constant touch with his mother, and she became convinced that he would be just fine. Clearly, he was not the one who had stepped over the parcel first. Miss Green saw Bernice every day. The girl was always cheerful and seemed to be in the best of health. She was beginning to think that the do-good man was no good, when Margaret turned up one evening.

"When las' you see your daughter-in-law?" she asked her.

"My daughter-in-law?" Rosa repeated. "But is what wrong wid dis woman, eh! You hear say Karl married?"

"Ansa mi, man. When las' you see her?" Margaret pressed.

"Who, Bernice?"

"Who else?"

Miss Green hesitated.

"Couple days now," she said. "Is what?"

"You don't hear say she sick?" Margaret asked.

Rosa's heart skipped a beat. Finally! Finally something was beginning to happen. She hid her excitement and asked with apparent concern, "So is what do her?"

"Mi hear say she weak an' can't eat, "Margaret replied.

"Well, well…I wonder what dat could be now."

"Mi hear say she goin' clinic tomorrow," Margaret said as she got up to leave. "Well I goin' now," she added. "Tek care."

"A'right, mi chile. T'ank you fo' dat piece o' news," Rosa said, without thinking.

Margaret gave her friend a puzzled look before she walked away.

Rosa remained seated long after her friend had left. She did not feel quite as happy as she thought she would have on the discovery that her plan was working. She reluctantly admitted to herself that she had begun to like Bernice a little. Pity, she was the wrong colour. But what was done was done. She roused herself and began to sing a chorus.

Two days later, she received a letter from Karl. The work was hard, he complained. The place was so cold that he was beginning to suffer pains in his back and legs. He had missed a few days' work, but the guys said he would become accustomed to the weather before long.

Late that night, Rosa heard a loud banging on the front door. She opened it to find Bernice standing there in tears.

"You hear from Karl, Ma'am?" Bernice asked.

"Is Karl you worryin 'bout now?" Rosa asked the girl. "I hear say you sick. What you doin' up here at dis hour of di night?" She then motioned for her to come in.

Bernice went inside the house. "One of my frien' husband jus call her. Him did go on farm work to, an' him say Karl sick bad over dere."

"But is today I hear from him an' him didn't tell me dat. I don't tek dat back problem too serious," Rosa told Bernice.

"Him have dat problem from him was a little boy. An' dat cold weather jus' meck matters worse. Him soon a'right again."

"So it happen to him a'ready?" Bernice asked.

"Yes. Him was only eight years ole when him drop off a guinep tree. Is dat cause it."

"Oh." Bernice wiped her tears away. "Mi feel so much betta now."

"So is what wrong wid you," Rosa asked. "Mi hear say you sick."

Bernice got up and moved to the door.

"I don't tink is anyting serious," she said evasively. "But mi not feelin' so good now so mi goin'."

"A'right mi dear. Walk good."

Bernice left and Miss Green returned to bed. She was not at all worried by the news that Karl was ill. He was a strong young man, and she felt sure that he would be okay. She slept peacefully that night.

The telegram came the following day. Its message was brief and brutal: KARL MACNEIL IS DEAD.

Many people in Cattle Ridge thought Rosa Green would lose her mind. Nothing passed her lips for close to a week. Her friends sympathized and grieved with her. They understood. What they didn't understand was why she blamed herself for the young man's death.

They tried to console her by telling her how good a mother she had been to Karl. But that only made her wish she was dead too. She came very close to telling all. She felt that the pain would become more bearable if she could tell somebody that she had unwittingly murdered her own son. In the interest of self-preservation she did not.

⊱✿⊰

A few days after the funeral, Bernice, weak from mourning, went to see Rosa, who had given little thought to the girl's existence since she had gotten the news of Karl's death. Once or twice, she had wondered briefly what had been wrong with Bernice.

"You did go back to docta?" she asked.

"Docta?"

"Yes. Dat problem you was havin'. You a'right now?"

"Oh, dat problem…Miss Green," Bernice continued quietly. "Mi have something to tell you."

"Oh? Is what dat now?"

"Mi did go back to docta an' him did say…"

"Say what? Talk up, man!"

"Him say mi pregnant. I believe it happen di week before Karl leave here."

The air was still as the two women stared at each other across the room. Then the tears came again. Rosa wept like a child as Bernice reached out to comfort her. Minutes passed. Rosa wiped her tears and asked, "Karl did know 'bout it?"

"No, Ma'am. By time mi fi tell him, him…" Bernice started crying again.

Rosa groaned. She tried to control herself.

"Nuh mine, mi dear," she said, her voice shaking a little. "Don't worry 'bout it. You can depend on mi to help you."

They clung to each other like two lonely survivors caught in the swell of a vile and vengeful storm.

PUSS FOOD

Benjamin Nelson was a quiet man. He owned one of the biggest farms in Cabbage Cut but still found time to read. Maas Benjy, as he was affectionately known, was a great admirer of famous philosophers whom he had come to know through the books his wife, Lynda, had brought into their marriage. But Maas Benjy now lived alone with his dog and his cat, Aristotle.

He loved animals. He felt he owed respect to all – man and beast – who had the "gumption" to be born into this "wicked world". Of all his animals, only Aristotle and his cow, Nurse, had the good fortune of being given names. Maas Benjy called his dog "Big Dog", and he avoided anybody he could not respect, so naturally he avoided Vicky.

Vicky was born in Cabbage Cut, married young and widowed early. Her husband, Jack, had died under "questionable circumstances" less than a week after asking her for a divorce. Vicky had several boyfriends after that, none of whom saw it fit to take her on a second trip to the altar. But she was a stubborn woman who was far from being ready to give up on the idea of owning a husband again.

Not only was Vicky a great cook, she was also very pretty. Even as a mature woman, her physical features remained superb. A boyfriend of hers had once remarked that the Creator must have spent more time making Vicky than He had on any other woman. But whether her Maker lived in heaven or was the occupant of a lower domain was debatable, because Vicky's voluptuous bosom seemed to cradle a heart that held the venom of seven big and deadly snakes.

Everybody in Cabbage Cut knew that Vicky had her eye on Benjy. What they didn't know was that she was busily making plans to take possession of the man, even when Lynda was still very much alive.

Lynda was never a strong person. But though she could not do a lot on the farm, she brought to Benjy's life the gentleness and peace which he never thought he would find in a woman. The fact that she was an intellectual simply made it sweeter. Sadly, Miss Lynda was forced to give up on having children after three miscarriages. She was never the same again.

Meanwhile, Vicky watched from a distance, waiting impatiently for the demise of her "rival". Finally, she decided she would have to speed up the process. Early one morning, she began the journey to meet with her favourite obeah man.

"Sista Vicky!" the man greeted her. "Long time no see! Come inside."

She went in.

"What you come 'bout now?" Carson Waite wanted to know.

He was a tall, lean man of about seventy and made a lucrative living from his practice of the magical arts. His head was wrapped in white and a white, toga-like garment covered most of his body.

"You know Benjy, Papa Waite?" Vicky asked. "Benjy Nelson from Cabbage Cut?"

"I know him. A simple lookin' man wid a big farm. I hear him wife have money."

"A she a mi problem!" Vicky spoke softly, but her tone was sinister.

"Problem?" Papa Waite was momentarily baffled. Then the light of understanding dawned in his beady little eyes. "Oh, a Benjy you want?"

Vicky nodded.

Waite smiled.

"So why you nevva say dat?" he asked. "You know Papa Waite can do anyting! But dat is a big, big job an' it goin cos' you, Sista."

Vicky dived into the bag she had brought with her. Her hand came up holding a thick wad of notes.

"Dis can do it?" she asked, handing over the money.

Waite took it, counted it and was pleased. He grinned broadly, exposing a mouthful of large, yellow teeth.

"Don't worry, Sista Vicky," he beamed. "Papa Waite goin' solve you problem."

***

Vicky cried like a crocodile at the funeral. Maas Benjy's grief was pitiful. He would have preferred even a helpless Lynda than no Lynda at all.

A few days later, Aristotle, big, black, sleek and appealing, walked out of nowhere and into Benjy's life. Nobody had seen this puss before and none could convince him that the animal had not been sent by his recently departed wife to comfort him in his dark hours of loneliness.

Miss Lynda died in late April. Vicky had had her heart set on a June wedding, but she was smart enough to allow the widower the time he needed to grieve. She vowed never to do business with slow-poke Waite again. As she bided her time, she convinced herself that everything would turn out well. After all, Benjy was lonely and she was pretty. Lynda had left Benjy money which she needed. She could cook and Benjy could not. So why worry? This wedding thing was already in the bag!

⚜

It was a Sunday afternoon, and Miss Vicky had prepared a splendid meal for Benjy. Her nephew Leon carried the basket of goodies, wrapped in a stiffly starched towel, on his head. Vicky walked behind him as they headed for Benjy's house.

The two found him waiting expectantly on his front porch with Aristotle on his lap. His gentle, calloused hand caressed the cat as he welcomed them with a wide grin.

"Evening, Miss Vicky!" he called as he saw them. "How di two a you doin'?"

"Not bad," Vicky replied. "Dis is mi nephew, Leon."

"How you doing, Missa Lee?"

Leon mumbled a response as the two climbed the steps to the porch. It was then that Vicky's eyes met Aristotle's. And it was mutual hate at first sight. For Benjy's benefit, she assumed a delightful smile and extended a hand to pet the puss.

"What a pretty likkle puss!" Vicky glowed. (Aristotle was a very large cat.) "Kitty, kitty, kitty!...What him name, Benjy?"

But Aristotle was no hypocrite. Before Benjy could reply, the cat responded by snarling loudly and viciously, baring his fangs and scaring the daylights out of the woman. Vicky's hand recoiled abruptly as she gasped and took a step backward.

"Behave youself, Puss!" Benjy yelled, throwing Aristotle to the floor. "What's wrong wid you, Aristotle?...But what a feisty puss!...A mad you mad?... Suppose you did scratch di lady? Come out a di place, man!...Mad puss!...An' don't come back!"

Aristotle walked leisurely away with his tail in the air, no apology in his demeanour.

Vicky smiled lovingly at Benjy. With the puss in the dog house, she chalked up her first victory against Aristotle and happily spread the feast for her future husband.

After she had left, Maas Benjy called Aristotle and scolded him again. Then he fed him what was left of the magnificent meal and Aristotle ate it vigorously.

The following Sunday, Miss Vicky had to attend a funeral so Leon brought Maas Benjy's dinner. Vicky loved funerals. She called them "dead party". Most people have to at least know somebody who knew the deceased for them to want to attend the funeral. Not Miss Vicky. All she needed to know was when and where it would take place. Vicky had four funeral frocks: One was black, one white, one purple and the fourth a mix of black, white and purple.

Having heard how much Aristotle had liked her cooking, she sent him his special portion in a shiny calabash. She had even scratched the name "Harry" on the calabash.

Maas Benjy was deeply touched by the gesture. He was relieved and happy that Vicky had so quickly forgiven Aristotle of his bad behaviour.

The food was beautiful. Vicky had outdone herself. Maas Benjy's "niggeritis" – a sign of deep satisfaction – had begun to kick in even before he finished eating. He slept deep and comfortably that Sunday evening.

❧

Later, at about eight o'clock, Benjy discovered that the cat had not touched his own dinner. Benjy warmed up the food in the calabash and proceeded to persuade the puss to partake. He tasted it a few times to demonstrate its virtue. But the cat could not be swayed.

If Aristotle could talk, he would have told his master that the food on the table was different from that in the calabash. The latter just didn't smell right. Had he not investigated the matter himself while Benjy was asleep? And while he was at it, he had helped himself to a goodly portion of the leftovers from the table. So he was fine.

Benjy eventually gave up and turned in for the night.

It would be necessary to stretch the imagination to its farthest limits in attempting to fathom the perils of Maas Benjy's bowels that night. The poor man nearly died. Never before had he and his toilet been closer. Aristotle watched helplessly.

Though nobody could prove that Vicky had anything to do with Miss Lynda's passing, her attempt on Aristotle's life was the talk of Cabbage Cut for months. Benjy never looked at her again, and her later attempts at snagging a husband proved fruitless.

About two years later, Leon's mother called him to her one day.

"When las' you see you Auntie?" she asked.

"'Bout...'bout three days now," Leon replied. "Is what?"

"Dis not like her at all," his mother said. "Everybody know how Vicky walk 'bout. Maybe you shoulda go check and see if she alright, Lee."

Leon went to his aunt's house. He got no response after knocking and calling for several minutes, so he climbed up and peeped through a window. From there, he could see the top of Vicky's head. She was sitting in a chair with her back to him.

"Auntie Vicky!" he called. "Is me, Leon. Open di door."

Vicky neither moved nor spoke, so the boy left to get help.

When the men eventually broke the door down, they saw something which would haunt their dreams for nights to come: Vicky was seated in an armchair with a sickening expression on her face. Her hair was all over the place; her eyes looked ready to pop out of her head, and her lips were pulled back almost to her ears in wild terror. Her hands clutched the arms of the chair, and the nightgown she had on was torn. The air in the room reeked of an unholy stench.

The coroner had a hard time determining the cause of death. In the end, it was ruled an "unnatural death"that had occurred under "questionable circumstances". Most people in Cabbage Cut still believe that Vicky's demise was the result of her having been visited by "something evil" of the supernatural order.

Vicky would have been pleased at the turnout at her own "dead party". Almost everybody, including Maas Benjy and Aristotle, were present. But though it was a big funeral, there was hardly a sad face in the place. For most people were there not to pay their respects but because they feared the duppy of the deceased.

They were at her graveside, singing the last song over Vicky, when Aristotle was heard making some rather curious noises. Benjy ignored the sounds, but Leon walked over to the cat.

"A bawl him a bawl fi mi auntie?" he asked.

Maas Benjy peered closely at the cat now perched on the boy's shoulder. Then he looked back at Leon.

"You can nevva tell wid a puss like dis," he concluded. "Maybe a laugh him a laugh."

MISS ESSIE AND THE DO-GOOD MAN

Mrs. Esther Wisdom owned the biggest shop in her district. The most imposing structure in the village square, it was a two-story building with Miss Essie's dwelling on the top floor and the shop below. This lady saw herself as the biggest and best Christian in Bowland. She stoutly and frequently condemned all who did not go to church or observe the Sabbath. She lived alone since her two grown daughters had moved away. A divorcée, Miss Essie was short and round – a dumpling of a lady.

Mr. Bradford (Bredda) Myrie – the resident obeah man – was, on the other hand, almost entirely free of fat. He was of average height and had a long, boney face with a usually sad expression. Bredda, who was a widower, may have been two or three years younger than Miss Essie.

The thought of a person like Bredda getting close to her would have sent Miss Essie's blood pressure sky-rocketing. For unlike the man who desired her from a distance, she could not accept the fact that love in its blind intensity would refuse to be side-tracked by anything as ordinary as religion or class status.

As treasurer of the Bowland Church of the Blessed Saints, Miss Essie knew all who did not put the required one-tenth in the envelope every Sunday. Whenever such a person would enter the shop, she would embark on her sermon of how wrong it was to be mean to the Lord, frequently concluding with the prophecy: "Woe unto all tight people when dem finally buck up God!"

Caleb Graham was a casual worker and the young man whom Miss Essie regarded as the most irreverent of all the "sinners" in Bowland.

"Miss Essie?"said Caleb, one day after overhearing the sermon.

"What you want?" the lady asked him. "You don't hear mi talkin', Caleb?"

"You evva see God a come a shop come spen' money yet?"

Miss Essie completely lost her cool. Angrily, she glared at Caleb and, not for the first time, loudly drove him out of her shop.

In this district, anybody who desired the services of a do-good man had no need for bus or taxi fare. Bredda's "headquarters" (as he called it) was no farther than a muddy mile away from the village square. He attracted clients from every corner of Jamaica, and his services did not come cheap. So why, the villagers argued, wouldn't he do something about the road leading to his business place?

Bredda's usually well-dressed clients always came armed with a pair of mud boots since their cars had to be left parked in the square. All the nice ladies who came clad in expensive pants or jeans had to roll them up to at least knee height, before descending to the headquarters. Long skirts had to be tied or pinned up. (Miss Essie always kept a ready supply of safety pins.) The male clients brought with them at least one pair of large (bicycle) clasps, which looked like metallic rings. These they would use to keep the cuffs of their pants hiked high up and safe from mud.

One day a very important businessman drove his Mercedes into Bowland. After taking all the precautions he thought necessary, he embarked on the arduous journey to Bredda's place. He had almost made it when he suddenly found himself face down in a smelly pool of stale mud. Mr. Businessman had fortitude, and he was back on his feet almost as quickly as he had lost his vertical position. He had come with a purpose, and he wasn't about to allow a little mud to distract him from his goal. If a man wanted good, as the saying went, his nose (and, in this case, his face) had to run.

So onward he trotted. He was eagerly ushered into the headquarters and Bredda's ladies-in-waiting began the regular task of returning to a state of plausible respectability a client who had taken a mud dive. But instead of restoring to the man his sense of decency, the women thoroughly ruined his new silk shirt. And the poor man finally lost it.

He proceeded to let fly a seemingly unending string of dirty words that came stuttering out of him like bullets from an automatic gun. The attendants ran for cover. From his inner sanctum, Bredda heard the commotion and, excusing himself from the client he was attending to, he came out to see what the fuss was about.

Mr. Businessman, who was still very hot under the collar, informed Bredda that he was nothing but a mean and stupid ole bush doctor, who was not even smart enough to fix the road leading to his place of business. "You are a rogue and a thief," he said, "and your only interest is in money!"

Bredda gazed at him in silence as the man continued to yell. "How," he asked, "could an educated man like myself have been misled into coming all the way from Kingston, to suffer the indignities I have had to today, just to seek assistance from a scoundrel like you?"

Bredda was deeply offended. This display was very bad for business. He had to do some damage control and fast. Bredda then proceeded to make a terrible spectacle of himself, frightening everybody except the man he was trying to mash up. Then he clasped his hands and, with head held high, he began to mumble an unintelligible malediction. In the midst of all this, the businessman suddenly crashed to the floor.

Bredda's mouth fell open as he stared at the man. He was startled by the potency of his own powers. Then he smiled. He had proven himself. He had destroyed the enemy! Once more he clasped his hands and bowed low to his clients. He did not turn when he heard the man cussing again. Shortly thereafter, the enemy strode noisily out of the place, scathingly denouncing Bredda's unreliable chairs.

"Just wait till I get back to town," he threatened. "You will hear from my lawyer if my back has been damaged!"

When Miss Essie heard the story, she shook her head.

"You see dat man, Bredda? Him is sure to come to a quick an' bitta end!" she said.

Sister Lizzy, who had brought her the story, totally agreed with this pronouncement. But she knew that

Bredda's clients did not generally like to travel with food and were usually hungry after their business transactions had been completed. In time, Miss Essie came to know exactly what they liked to eat, and she made sure she always had in stock the dry food and drinks the sojourners from the headquarters may desire.

"Is jus' a pity," Sister Lizzy noted, "dat if him dead or stop work obeah, certain tings wha fi him customer dem buy from you woulda stop sell."

Miss Essie said nothing, but she was visibly worried. She hadn't thought of that. Minutes later she asked her friend to take two aspirins from the shelf for her and get her some water. Miss Essie had suddenly developed a headache which was giving her a 'warm time'.

❦

The day eventually came when Miss Essie fell sick. None of the several doctors she visited was of any help. She was finally confined to bed, and one of her daughters came to help her. The sisters from church began to encourage Miss Essie to "go and look". Sister Lizzy's husband told her that he knew a good man in St. Mary, and he would take her there free of charge. All she had to give him was gas money.

While Miss Essie pondered the matter, Bredda, being the good neighbour he thought himself to be, decided to call on her. The visit was unexpected, and Miss Essie came close to a stroke when she heard that Bredda was sitting on her verandah waiting to see her. He heard as she commanded her daughter, "Drive dat devil off a mi property!"

It was late in the day when everybody was home and a crowd had begun to gather. Reactions were mixed. Some felt that Bredda had passed his place since he knew well what Miss Essie thought of him and his obeah. Others felt that she could have at least received him, being the big Christian she was. They all knew that Bredda truly loved Miss Essie and that if the circumstances had been different, he might even have dared to pop the question.

Bredda was undaunted. As he rose to depart, he told the crowd that all he wanted was to help his neighbour. Then he shocked them all by beginning to quote from the prophet Isaiah. Most people didn't even think that Bredda owned a Bible. Bredda told them with ceremony, "A good man is always 'despised and rejected', as di prophet say!" His left hand rested piously upon his chest, he was the 'good man'.

"But more dan di Lord Jesas," he continued, "Bredda Myrie is 'rejected' not just by 'men' but by many inna dis place!"

Then, without preamble, he drew a bottle from his pocket, quickly sprinkled its contents around Miss Essie's front door and began a strange chant. The crowd gasped. The smell of the oil was revolting, like cow dung mixed with garlic. Miss Essie's daughter needed to do nothing to get rid of the intruder as the throng, by threats and insults, quickly drove him away.

Bredda was not many yards down his muddy decline, when Miss Essie began to vomit. The smell of the oil seemed to have affected her. She had to be rushed away to the new doctor in town. (Miss Essie did not trust new doctors. She preferred to wait and see whether or not anybody would die after visiting such a doctor, before she entrusted her life to him or her.)

Caleb was itching to ask Miss Essie why she was so reluctant to leave this "wicked earth", as she called it, if her place in heaven was so secure. But he decided to wait till she was better. The patient was too sick to object, so the new doctor did his job without hindrance. Everybody had gone to bed by the time she got back home that night.

Hardly anybody was as surprised as her when Miss Essie got out of bed all on her own the following morning. Most people couldn't believe it was the same woman who was up and about and doing her business as usual. Caleb was so delighted to see her functioning as her old self again that he couldn't help saying what was in his heart:

"I did know say Bredda wasn't a bad man," he glowed. "Look how much doctor you try eh, Miss Essie? Mi so glad say him help you fi get all a dat bad stuff off a you stomach."

Miss Essie stopped what she was doing and looked hard at Caleb.

"Tek you big, long foot dem out a mi shop!" she commanded.

"But mi was jus' a say...."

"You hear mi, Caleb?" Miss Essie interrupted. "Is di new docta help mi. So stop talk nonsense an' go do you work."

"How you so sure say is not Bredda?"

"Don't argue wid mi, Caleb Graham!"

"But…"

"Stop you 'buttin' an' butt outa mi life! An' don't come back!"

Caleb sauntered away. He was trying to decide who was really responsible for making Miss Essie well again. It was a difficult thing to figure out so he gave the benefit of the doubt to Bredda. Then he began to wonder when Miss Essie would get tired of running him out of her shop. It wasn't like she didn't know he would come back.

>~~🌼~~

Bredda was very happy to hear of Miss Essie's recovery. He, of course, credited himself for the speedy and dramatic change in the lady's health situation. He was most pleased to have been able to help his lady, and his confidence grew. The following Friday, Bredda came to the shop. He could not rely on his attendants to do his shopping, he said, so he had to come himself at least once a week. Miss Essie walked out the moment she saw him walk in, leaving Jenny (her assistant) to attend to him. Bredda was not deterred.

In time, Jenny began to notice that although Miss Essie continued to disappear whenever Bredda came to the shop, she would always come back before he left. Her hair would be nicely combed up and she had powdered her face. She would pretend not to see Bredda till he greeted her and told her how nice she looked. Miss Essie would hiss her teeth and pretend to be annoyed, but Jenny could see that she liked the compliments.

When Caleb became aware of this new development, he asked, "Why you playin' hard to get, Miss Essie? Tek di man! You believe you a go get any younger?"

Miss Essie drove him out of the shop.

Bredda soon learned from hard, personal experience that it was necessary for him to fix his road so he did. This should have helped his business, but his frequent visits to Miss Essie's shop caused him to fall behind in his work, and he began to lose a few of his clients.

Caleb was coming from work one day when he saw Bredda sitting in Miss Essie's shop. He was leaning on the far end of the counter and gazing in silence at his beloved.

"Is wha' you a waste time a Miss Essie shop a look inna her face fo' man?" he asked. "You don't have nutten a you yard fi do?"

Miss Essie was outraged.

"But, Lawd, tek di case!" she exclaimed. "Is when you goin' to learn fi mind yuh own business, Caleb?"

Caleb ignored her and turned to Bredda again.

"You know say I jus' meet up two a you customer dem a ask fi you? Go look 'bout you business, man! You believe say Miss Essie a go feed you when you hungry?"

"Come out a mi shop, Caleb!" Miss Essie shouted. "Somebody musta set you pon mi. Come out! Now, now, now !"

But he was not done counselling Bredda, who was listening without a word.

"Everyday you a fret over dis woman who don't care one biscuit 'bout you!" Caleb scolded. "Look how much nice young lady me see a come down deh to you. Is one a dem you mus' tek! Miss Essie is a ole, ole lady now."

This was too much. Even Bredda was insulted. Had he been a knight, he would have drawn a sword on behalf of his lady. Miss Essie's rage knew no bound. She was speechless. The moment was poignant with mixed emotions. And the Devil took a hold of the spirit-filled woman.

Before Jenny realized what she was about to do, Miss Essie reached up, took a large tin of sardines from the shelf and threw it at Caleb's head. The lady's aim was perfect, but Caleb saw the sardine flying toward him and ducked just in time. The missile missed its intended target, but it caught Bredda full in the face. He fell to the floor. His mouth was bleeding, and there was a large gash in the back of his head where it had hit the floor.

"Lawd, have mercy!" Jenny screamed, running around to the front of the shop where Bredda lay.

"Him dead?" Miss Essie asked in a frightened voice.

Caleb and Jenny were kneeling over the unfortunate Bredda as they called his name, fanned and tried to revive him.

"Bring a bottle a bay rum, Sista Essie!" Jenny commanded.

Miss Essie quickly obeyed, peering over the shoulders of the two. Bredda opened his eyes.

"T'ank God!" Miss Essie said with relief. "You have to go carry him home, Caleb."

Caleb pulled himself up to his towering height and looked down at Miss Essie.

"Bredda can't leave here now," he told her.

"What! So where him goin' stay?"

"In a one a dem whole heap a bed wha you have here. You don't see say di man get a bad, bad lick? Him head cut to, you know! An' is you lick him."

"But is you cause it," Miss Essie told him. "You suppose to take responsibility for what you…"

Caleb cut her off. "Miss Essie, you see if you don't help Bredda today, I goin report you! Look wha' you do to di man? Him can dead you know. An' if him dead, you goin' get charge fi murda!"

And so it was that Bredda had his dream fulfilled at least in a small way. He slept at Miss Essie's house for close to two weeks. Miss Essie saw it as her penance to nurse him back to health. And as she cared for him, she could do nothing to prevent herself from beginning to care about him.

They are now good friends, but it is not likely that they will ever wed. Bredda will not stop working obeah, and it would just not look right for a cornerstone of the church like Miss Essie to marry a man who made his living from dabbling daily and deeply in evil. Only Caleb might be able to come up with a solution to this problem. But this person's health is now seriously at risk.

"Obeah Caleb and meck him dumb! Jus' fi a week or two…Teach him a lesson, man! Meck him learn fi stay out a people business," Miss Essie told Bredda.

But Bredda refuses; he argues that Caleb is a kind person who really means no harm. But love is strong and who knows when he might give in and decide to render poor Caleb speechless? Only time will tell.

DADDY

The branches of the elegant palms swayed in the breeze. Gentle blue waves flirted playfully with the soft white sand at the base of the palm trees. The sun beamed warmly down on those frolicking and sunbathing on the beach, as business went on as usual in the streets of the town. Now and then the voices of peddlers touting their wares could be heard over music in the barrooms. This was Landings, a modest little seaside town on the northern border of the county of Surrey.

Much of the town's income was earned from the tourist trade. And like many such sunny, fun-filled places, it also came with the shady trappings of drugs, gun running and prostitution. Devon McDonald and Ruby Jones were among the residents of Landings. Unlike others, like the school teachers, land owners, George Dunn and Sandra Bernard, who were either upper-middle or lower-middle class, Devon and Miss Ruby were born poor.

Devon's aspirations to become a daddy started at about the same time he came to the conclusion that his own father was no daddy at all. He would be a wonderful father, Devon told himself, assigning his family first place in his life. Not rum, tobacco or ganja. He would not be like his father who wasted his money on feminine sellers of sin while hungry worms gnawed at the guts of his children.

Devon was the oldest of four. The family lived in a small wooden house. He was only ten when he started selling bag juice to supplement the family's meagre income. Two years later, he had erected a crude little stall close to their home, from which his mother sold biscuits, sweets, oranges and other simple food items during the day time. Devon worked at the stall in the evenings. Before he left school, he began selling barbecued chicken from a drum on a popular street corner in town. When he opened the smallest restaurant in Landings, Carlene Dunn became his first employee.

It was from Carlene's father, George, that Devon bought most of the meat he used. George owned a chicken farm. He admired Devon's industriousness and encouraged the union between the young man and his daughter.

Kelly McDonald was the first child born to them. Whenever he found the time, Devon would watch his daughter from a distance, wondering how an ordinary person like himself could have contributed to the creation of such a delicately marvelous creature.

They were alone together for the first time when Kelly began yelling her head off. Apprehensively, Devon approached the crib and extended a wary hand. By this time, the baby was becoming very impatient so she grabbed hold of his finger and yelled some more. Before he knew it, Devon was changing his daughter. The job was not a perfect one, but

Kelly did not complain. She found comfort in his strong arms. His funny noises made her laugh. As soon as she could manage it, Kelly thought, she would instruct him to talk sense.

"You soon goin' need extra help you know," said Carlene to Devon one evening as they cleaned up.

"Why?" Devon asked. "You tired?"

"Of course! You don't tired? An' is time mi go tek Kelly from Miss Ruby, too."

"Mi wi finish off," Devon told her. "You go sit down meanwhile."

She sat at one of the tables, looking at him.

"Miss Ruby can cook, you know, Devon," Carlene said. "She used to cook a school long time."

"Mi know," Devon replied. "Don't is shortly afta she tek Kevin she stop?"

"Yes. Poor likkle Kevin!"

"But she takin' good care a him," Devon said. "Is a nice little boy. Pity him daddy did haffi dead like dat."

"You did know Lloyd good?"

"Miss Ruby son? Yeah man. Me an' him was in school di same time. From dem time deh him did want to be a policeman."

"Poor man! Well at least him die in di line o' duty, so Miss Ruby can get something from government fi Kevin."

"Yes, dat good," Kevin agreed, mopping furiously away.

"But you still might haffi hire her, Devon. Cause mi pregnant again."

❦

The evening after Brian McDonald was born Kelly asked, "You see di baby, Daddy?"

"Yes," Devon replied. "Him ugly you see, Kel!"

He laughed till he almost choked.

"Daddy," Kelly scolded, "You shouldn't be callin' my brodda 'ugly'! "

"Is my son to," Devon said. "An' I glad fi him. But wait till you see him face!"

When Carlene brought their son home the following day, Devon said to Kelly, "You see what I was tellin' you 'bout?"

"Yes," the child told her father. "But I love him. Maybe is because him look jus' like you!"

Devon's face dropped. Solemnly he told his daughter, "You mus' have manners to big people you know, girl."

"But is you tell mi to speak di truth," Kelly said, a devilish smile tugging at the corners of her mouth.

❦

Miss Ruby was at the counter one day when Sandra Bernard walked in. As usual, she was scantily dressed and wearing too much makeup and fake jewellry.

Slut! Miss Ruby said to herself. Out loud she asked, "What you need, Miss?"

"What I need?" Sandra asked, striking an attitude. "I need you fi tell you grandson fi stop tell lie pon Bruce."

Miss Ruby had no idea what she was talking about and said so.

"Him an' him frien' dem go tell Mr. Williams say Bruce smokin' a school and now him get suspension!"

Mr. Williams was the principal of the Landings School. Devon heard her from the back and came to enquire what was happening. Sandra repeated what she had told Miss Ruby. Then she added, "Is grudgeful cause it; none a dem nuh like Bruce cause him betta off dan dem!"

"Dat is not di point right now, Miss…" Devon started to say.

"Of course it is di point!" Sandra exploded. "Bruce look betta, him dress betta an' him daddy a 'Merica soon sen fi him…A grudge di whole a dem grudge mi son!"

"Tek it easy, Miss Sandra," Devon said. "Where is Kevin now, Miss Ruby?"

"Him suppose to be home wid him book," Miss Ruby said.

Sandra hissed derisively, muttering, "Like him can read nutten!"

"You know where Bruce is, Miss Sandra?"

"No," she replied. "You expect mi fi watch him all di time, Devon? But I know him wasn't smokin'."

"You sure?"

"But a wha you a cross question mi fah, sah?" Sandra asked. "Is a restaurant you have here or a courthouse? I wasn't dere! But I still don't want anybody carryin' news pon mi boy fi hinder him progress."

"I wi talk to Kevin 'bout it," Miss Ruby promised.

Sandra turned her back on them and stormed out of the restaurant without another word. The two watched her go.

"Bright and feisty!" Miss Ruby fumed. "A long time she hate mi you know. She did a look Lloyd one time, but him nevva want her, so she feel say a me did turn him 'gainst her."

"But mi nevva did know dat," Devon said.

"Plenty people nevva know," Miss Ruby said. "An' she don't even sure say di chile not smokin'. Maybe a she him get cigarette from to!"

"A 'Merica Bruce daddy live?"

"So mi hear," the elderly woman told her boss. "Is a tourist who did come a Landings one time. Nobody don't even sure him a di boy daddy."

"Wha?"

"Sandra wild like deer you know!"

Devon told Miss Ruby to be careful. The he suggested that what Bruce needed most was a father to guide him.

Miss Ruby was in agreement. "An' since a mi a Kevin daddy now," she said. "Watch mi an' him when I reach home!"

***

At age sixteen, Kelly managed to fall in love with a boy and out of favour with her father at the same time. Bruce Findlay, Sandra's son, appeared to be even more impressed by his own fine feathers than anybody else in Landings. While other students regarded the lack of a pen or notebook as a drawback, Bruce considered the lack of a comb or mirror as a tragedy of astronomical proportions. So when

Kelly came first, second or third in her class, Bruce would come third-last, second-last or dead last in his class.

To say that Devon did not like Bruce was to speak rather mildly of that situation. Before he realized that Kelly had liked off Bruce, he had regarded him as a shallow but harmless little fellow. But when it came to the matter of the capturing of his little girl's heart by that little pea-brained toy soldier, that was a horse of a totally different colour.

He had first spoken to Bruce at the restaurant. The business had expanded and he had hired more staff. His family had just moved into their own home, and Carlene now spent most of her time there. Devon had just installed a game machine at the suggestion of his father-in-law. He didn't much like that sort of thing, but Mr. Dunn had suggested that it would attract younger customers, and he trusted the older man's judgement.

"A Sandra pretty bwoy dat, Devon!" Miss Ruby whispered the first day he walked in.

"Bruce?"

She nodded.

Devon had a general idea what the boy looked like, but had never seen him up close. He looked at him, admitting to himself that he really was a handsome kid. He was about Kelly's age, give or take a year. Bruce's facial features mirrored his mother's, but his hair was curly and his skin colour lighter. He was tall for his age and carried well the fancy clothes he wore, though his cowboy boots seemed a bit out of place.

The girl with him was obviously thrilled to be in his company, as was every other girl he brought with him in the weeks that followed. Bruce couldn't get enough of the new machine.

"A weh him get so much money?" Devon asked Miss Ruby.

"I don't even know," Miss Ruby confessed. "But mi hear say him a move wid di man who did involve inna mi son killin'."

"Wha! But nuh drugs man dat?"

Miss Ruby nodded. "But wha else him fi do?" she asked. "Sandra nah teach him nutten good."

"Well as long as him don't bring none a dem tings in here…"

But Devon soon began to detest the boy's superior attitude toward his friends, which his staff also had to put up with from time to time. He spoke to him the day he saw Bruce lighting up a cigarette.

"No smokin'," Devon said, pointing to the sign on the wall.

"You talkin' to me?" the boy asked.

"Is you alone smokin'."

"Jus' cool, man!" Bruce replied, smiling.

He took another drag.

"Put it out or get out!" Devon said firmly.

Their eyes met and held, but Bruce looked away first. Angrily he rose, overturning the chair he had been sitting on and cursing under his breath.

"I can't wait fi my Daddy sen' fi mi," were his parting words. "Tired a dem likkle fool-fool place yah, man!"

His cowboy boots squeaked an applause as he strode manfully out of the building.

"Good riddance!" Miss Ruby said to his back. "You nuh haffi come back."

⚘

Kelly heard Devon telling her mother the story. But as far as Miss Kelly McDonald was concerned, her father was making a big deal over nothing. Bruce wasn't perfect, but then who was? Neither was he the brightest card in the pack, but who cared? His looks made up for it, and she had enough brains for both of them anyway. She was perfectly capable of choosing her own friends.

A few weeks before her seventeenth birthday, Kelly decided to trick her parents into sending her on a date with Bruce. She knew it would take careful planning. Devon was watching her like a bull dog these days. When her father came home that Wednesday evening, she greeted him cheerfully.

"Hi, Daddy."

"Hi, Ma'am, how you doin'?" Devon replied.

"Fine."

She gave him a hug and a little kiss. Devon was suspicious. It had been a while since she had shown him such affection.

"So, Daddy, how was your day?" she asked.

"Okay. How was yours?"

"Great. Somebody ask mi out."

Devon turned to face his daughter. "I know you was up to something," he said.

"Me, Daddy?"

101

" 'Me, Daddy, Me Daddy'! " he mimicked her in a high-pitched voice.

"Easy nuh, Dads," Kelly said. "You want mi make you a drink?"

"No, I want you tell mi who you plannin' to go out wid."

"Why you getting so excited, Daddy?"

"Kelly," Devon said. "I ask you a question an' if you don't answer me right now I goin' slap you dis evening."

Kelly was taken aback.

"But I am a young lady now," she objected.

"Nevva too late for a shower o' rain! Tell me who you goin' out wid."

"Kevin," Kelly said.

"Kevin? Miss Ruby Kevin?"

"Yes, Daddy"

Devon liked and was proud of Kevin. His 'daddy', Miss Ruby, had done a great job with him. The boy had turned into a decent, hardworking teenager, who was doing very well at school. Devon sat down and pulled his daughter to him. He was smiling broadly.

"Is Kevin you want to go out wid, Kel ?" he asked.

"Yes, Daddy,"

"So why you didn't tell mi long time? Kevin is a fine, dependable boy. Of course, you can go out wid him."

"Thanks."

He patted her head and asked, "So where you planning to go?"

"Party at a friend house Saturday evening."

"Nice. So you dump di boots!" Devon said suddenly.

"Boots? What you talkin' about?"

"Di face boy, man. Is 'Boots' him name or 'Brute'?" Devon asked, laughing at his own joke.

Kelly watched him, disguising her annoyance with a stiff little smile. Why was he always putting Bruce down?"

"You mus' tell wi di exact time an' place you goin'," Devon then said.

"Okay."

"An' make sure you carry you own money."

"Yes, Daddy, thanks."

Saturday evening came. Kelly spent hours getting dressed. Carlene asked if she needed her help, but she told her she was managing alright. When she was done, Kelly was as hot as a country fire-side in July. She told her mother that she was going to a party with Kevin and that Devon knew all about it. She had planned things with the foresight that her father would not be home when she was ready to leave.

Devon came in about an hour later. Kelly had told him she would be leaving at seven o'clock, and he liked to see his daughter all dressed up. He was very disappointed that she had already left. He had wanted to drive her to meet Kevin. Devon decided to spend the rest of the evening at home with his wife and son.

Not much later, Miss Ruby called.

"Hi, Miss Ruby," Devon answered. "How you doin'?"

"Mi a'right. Is Kevin ask me to call you."

"Kevin?"

"Yes," Miss Ruby said. "Him ask me fi tell you say him not goin' able fi cut di yard fi you again. Him have a little flu an' him haffi prepare fi exam Monday to."

"Is what you sayin to mi, Miss Ruby? Kevin gone out wid my Kelly over one hour ago."

Miss Ruby was at a loss for words.

"A wha you a drink, Devon?" she asked. "Kevin is right here wid mi."

Devon said goodbye to her and hung up in a daze.

"What happen?" Carlene asked.

"Is not Kevin that Kelly gone out wid," he told her.

"What? So is who?"

"Maybe is Bruce," Brian suggested.

"You could be right," his father told him.

Carlene was shocked.

"But what a bad likkle gal!" she exclaimed.

Devon called Kelly's cell phone, but it was turned off.

"I haffi try find her," he said, heading toward the door.

He was very worried as he got into his pickup and took off in the direction he hoped his daughter had gone.

***

At about the same time, Bruce and Kelly were cruising into the location of the dance they had planned to attend. He was driving his mother's car. Kelly was ecstatic that she had finally managed this date with Bruce. It had taken careful planning but the reward was sweet. She smiled happily across at him. All this guy needed, she was thinking, was a wise woman like herself to guide him. She was sure she could convince him to stop his womanizing ways and settle down to some serious living. Her father would then have no reason to reject him.

Bruce smiled back at her. This was his long overdue opportunity. Kelly would be his tonight. He had no intention of getting her pregnant; he wanted nobody but himself to take care of. Besides, if anything like that were to happen, Devon would not stop chasing him till he had caught him and squeezed the last bubble of air from his body.

"My girl," he said softly.

"Yes, Bruce?"

"What time you bone-head daddy want you home?"

"What? Don't call him dat. He is just protective."

"A'right. What time your 'protective' daddy want you home?"

"Ten-thirty."

"Ten-thirty? But is seven o'clock now."

"Right. So we can dance till ten o'clock an' leave."

"Kelly," Bruce said smoothly. "You are a big girl now, you know."

"I know I am a big girl."

"Well…" He hesitated. "We can dance till nine o'clock an' leave."

"Why?"

"Kelly, you don't like mi?"he asked.

"Of course. What kinda fool-fool question dat! Why you tink I go through so much trouble to come wid you tonight?"

Bruce flicked open the glove compartment.

"I not plannin' to get you in trouble," he said. "I have protection. I always travel wid my boots!"

"Is what dat?" Kelly asked, looking closer.

She looked and saw and understood. Condoms. Her father had been right all along, and it made her angry to have to admit it to herself. This boy had serious designs on her body. She was such a fool to have been taken in by his good looks.

"Bruce," she said quietly. "Stop di car."

"What? But we almost reach."

"Stop dis car now!"

"A'right." He pulled over. "What happen?"

"Is trick I trick my parents into allowin' me to come out wid you," Kelly said, "An' is dis sorta slackness you have on your mind? Daddy was right about you! You try find somebody else to kick wid you boots, because I am not dat person!"

Bruce was exasperated.

"You an' your daddy come like idiot!" he said.

"You hear mi say you not to call him any name?"

"I fed up wid di two o' you!"

"Me fed up to," Kelly told him. "So jus' turn dis car round an' take mi back to mi yard."

"I not takin' you anywhere," Bruce said. "If you want to go, open di door an' gwan!"

Kelly looked calmly at him.

"Who you want me to call firs'," she asked. "Mi daddy or police?"

"Police! What I do you for you to be callin' police?"

"I goin' to call mi daddy den!"

"A'right, you win!" Bruce shouted.

He spun the car around and drove like only a frustrated man could. The two sped along in a tense silence, which was broken only by the screeching of the tires. Kelly was anxious to get home, so she wasn't about to let Bruce know that she was more than a little scared by his erratic driving. She gritted her teeth as the wind made a mess of her hair.

As they rounded the bend at the entrance to the Landings' town square, Bruce's car and Devon's pickup crashed into each other. The noise was deafening. There was glass everywhere, and Bruce was slumped over the steering wheel. Kelly was screaming hysterically.

Thankful that he was not hurt, Devon jumped out and ran to his daughter. He managed to get the car door open.

"Hush, baby," he said. "Daddy goin' take care o' you, you hear? You soon a'right again."

Gently he placed her inside the pickup and went back to check on Bruce. The boy was unconscious but still breathing. Two other motorists had come onto the scene, and they helped him get Bruce out and take both youngsters to the hospital.

When Sandra arrived, she was her usual melodramatic self, crying and fawning all over Bruce and getting in the way of the hospital staff. After they had shooed her away, she promptly began to blame Kelly for what had happened and told Devon he would have to pay for the damage to her car. Devon told her to stop talking rubbish. Sandra said she was just happy that Bruce's father would be sending for him soon, so he could get away from all the worthless people in Landings. Ready to take his daughter home,

Devon replied that he wished that great day would come in a hurry so he could finally stop hearing about it.

⟞⟝❀⟞⟝

When Kelly woke up the following day, only Devon was at home. He was sitting at the table when she walked into the dining room.

"Where Mom an' Brian, Daddy?" Kelly asked.

"You madda and Brian at di restaurant," Devon told her.

"How you feelin'?"

"Not too bad. Only weak."

"Come eat something so you can feel betta."

She sat down with him and asked, "You hear anyting 'bout Bruce, Daddy?"

"Him wake up a'right," Devon said. "But him might not be such a ladies' man anymore."

"What you mean?"

"Him face get some bad cut."

"Poor Bruce!"

"Is what really happen between you two las' night?" Devon asked. "How di two a you come back so soon?"

"Nothing. Jus' di accident."

"You sure, Kelly?"

"Nothing happened, Daddy. Bruce was plannin' on getting lucky but…"

"What!"

"Yes, I was so wrong about him. Sorry."

Devon gazed in silence at his daughter. Then he said,

"Your Missa Boots luckier dan him will evva know! You get you punishment in dat accident fi trying to fool me an' Carlene, Kelly. But if dat boy ever come near you again, him not goin' to be able to wear any kinda boots, neither pon him foot or anywhere else!"

VALERIE'S REVENGE

When Chad came into the world, he was not exactly welcome. At least not by his mother, Inez Burrows. Inez, the fun-crazed, party-all-the-time type, was a beautiful woman. She had married Alvin only because he worked hard and was free with his money. Alvin was a construction worker who lived in the country town of Lebanon. He was tall and thin with prominent eyes in a solemn face. But his countenance may have belied his temperament. For Alvin could take a joke as well as he could give one, and especially so after he had had a few under his belt. The couple's house could proudly hold its head up among the others in Lebanon, simply because Inez refused to quit nagging Alvin until he had completed it. This man was all heart, comfortable with himself and everybody else. The spirit of competition was as foreign to his nature as profanity is to the lips of a saint.

If Inez had discovered in time that she was pregnant, Chad would never have been born. She found out late and was a little nervous about doing the abortion. She had had this procedure done before but never so late in the pregnancy.

She communicated her feelings to Alvin who was dead set against the idea. It wasn't that Alvin was particularly attracted to the idea of being a father. He liked children, but he doubted that he had what it took to cope with such a responsibility. Like everybody else in Lebanon, Alvin knew he was a little too fond of booze. But he had a deep respect for life and was very much opposed to his wife's destroying a life, which he himself had a part in creating.

"You mad?" he asked his wife. "Why you want to destroy di firs' chile me an' you goin' have, Inez? An' maybe kill off youself to!"

Inez gave him a pitiful look. Poor Alvin, she thought.

So Chad was born, and Inez left before he was a year old. He was cramping her style, she said. Alvin buckled down to the business of raising his son. He stopped drinking hard and found that he had all it took to be both father and mother to the boy.

Alvin worked mostly with Luther Byles. The two had been friends from school days. They had even been in the same class at one time. But Luther was no small-fry workman like Alvin. He was a big contractor who could build a palace if he felt inclined to. Luther was a tall, thick-set man who dressed well and drove a Jaguar – the type most women find attractive. When he was young he had them in droves. Now, in the prime of his life, Luther cultivated the lifestyle he thought people would look up to and admire – lavishly successful but very respectable. Joan, his trophy wife, was a big part of this image. Luther lived with her in a big, beautiful house on the edge of town.

After many years of working with Luther, Alvin attained permanent status. This had nothing to do with the quality of his work. He just happened to be in the right place at the right time and to see something which was altogether wrong. The place was the site of one of Luther's bigger projects. The building had been commissioned by a Mr. Rupert Lindsay, who had spent most of his working life in England. Mr. Lindsay was to return to this house in Jamaica to pass his winter years under the golden sun of his native land. The time was late one Friday night after Alvin had left the bar and was heading home. Chad had been left with an aunt who had come to visit, while his father was having a night on the town with friends.

Alvin saw the faint light among the trees and wondered who the devil could be at the work site at that time of the night. Maybe it was somebody trying to steal something. He changed course and went closer. Then he saw Luther.

Look like him have a gal-frien', Alvin said to himself.

He had no intention of disturbing him, but he just had to see who Luther was messing with now. He moved quietly closer. Why didn't the man choose a better place for his night-time carryings-on? From the cover of the bushes, Alvin saw Luther carrying a bucket. Something did not seem quite right. He edged closer.

As Alvin watched, Luther lifted a girl and placed her in the newly dug foundation. Alvin blushed. Maybe he should leave. Then his mouth dropped wide open as Luther began to empty the bucket of mortar in the same spot he had placed the girl.

"Luta!" Alvin yelled.

Luther jerked to a pause, the half-empty bucket still in his hand. Alvin walked out of the darkness.

"Is what you doin' man?" Alvin asked, moving closer. "Is who dat?"

Luther had dug what looked like a shallow grave in the already done excavation.

"Luta, answer mi man! Is who you put down dere so?...Why she not sayin' anyting?"

Luther finally recovered himself.

"Is Gooden daughta," he said.

"What! You mean Valerie?"

"Yes." Luther's voice was cold and flat like the girl on the ground. "She dead."

"But what is dis now!"

"Is a accident, Alvin. Mi didn't mean to harm her."

"What happen?" Alvin asked.

Luther sighed heavily. He placed the bucket on the ground.

"Afta she take mi money," he said, "she start gwan like she bad."

"So is dat why you kill her?"

"No, no! It was a accident, mi tell you." Luther spoke with feeling now. "Is pull she a pull way from mi when she drop an' lick her head."

"What a hell! So is wha' you a do now? Is here you plan to bury her?"

"What else I mus' do?"

"But you mad!" Alvin exclaimed. "You can't do dat... You can't do dat, man!"

"What else mi mus' do?" Luther asked again.

"You can report it an' explain youself," Alvin suggested. "You can afford to get a good lawyer. Don't you say is a accident?"

"Mi not goin' get way wid dis, Alvin," Luther said gloomily. "Everybody goin' believe say is me kill her."

"But you can't bury her like dis," Alvin objected. "You can't handle it like dis, man. It jus' not right."

"So it right fi me go a prison because o' one little accident?"

"Little accident'?" Alvin echoed. "Little accident? Di girl dead, man! Is not a puss kitten you dealin' wid here you know, Luta! Is a person!"

"I done explain di whole ting to you a'ready, but I sure nobody goin' believe mi." Luther shook his head. "Is mash my life mash up now!" he said. "An' I am a person to."

Alvin was silent. Finally he said, "I don't know what to say 'bout dis now."

"You know as well as me say dis is my only way out ah dis mess," Luther said.

"So what 'bout when dem start search fi her?" Alvin asked.

"Everybody know say she was a little bad gal. People wi' jus' say she run way."

"You is a hard man, Luta! I didn't know you coulda do a ting like dis."

"But you see say mi can't do anyting else. You goin' help mi, Al?"

"Help you? You mad!"

"So you goin' report mi den?"

"I can't judge you," Alvin said, slowly. "I goin' keep you secret though I don't like it at all. But you goin' finish dis ting here without me." He turned to go. "I have to go home to Chad."

"Thank you, Al," Luther was relieved. "You goin' always have a job wid mi now!"

Then Alvin turned back. "How you plan to hide dis from di rest o' work man dem tomorrow?" he asked Luther.

"Don't worry 'bout dat man," Luther answered. "Me wi' jus' tell dem say mi sick an' work haffi stop fi a few days."

"You have everyting work out fine, eh?"

"Have to!" Luther said, his gaiety returning. His friend's sarcasm was lost on him.

"Me an' you a frien' from we little," Alvin continued. "But I didn't know you at all, Luta! I didn't know you woulda have di guts fi do a ting like dis."

Alvin walked away.

❧

Luther's son Steven was born three months after Chad. He was a chubby, dark-skinned boy with a friendly disposition. Chad was slender and a bit more reserved, with his father's eyes. The boys were inseparable. They played together, got into mischief together, fought and made up together.

It was Chad who first called Steven "Fatty". When they had tired from thumping and kicking each other in the dirt, each got up to go home. Steven was busy dusting himself off and thinking that he had surely taught Chad a lesson when he heard it again: "Fat, fat, Fatty!" Chad was saying. "Fatty fatty, baby!"

Steven hurled a stone at Chad and yelled, "Shut up, Bug Eye!"

Chad had never been called a nickname, but he was not offended. The fat boy had spunk!

"A'right. I won't call you Fatty again, Fatty!" he said laughing.

Like their friendship, the nicknames stuck.

Chad was about eight years old when he began to wonder about the relationship between Luther and his father. Mr. Byles was very serious about keeping up appearances. Respectable behaviour seemed very important to him. Yet, Chad noticed that he was always closest to Alvin when the latter was drunk. Alvin had started drinking hard again since the night of Valerie's "burial". Inez's filing for divorce did not help matters either. Every man in Lebanon knew Alvin's song. He always sang it when he was very, very drunk.:

Valerie Gooden, whey you gone
Valerie Gooden, whey you is
Oh, Valerie Gooden!
Valerie Gooden, where you is
Valerie Gooden, what you did
Oh, Valerie Gooden!

At first people were amused. Alvin had talent! They were amazed. Then they began to wonder. At such times, Luther would become visibly uneasy. But in quick time, he learned to detract attention from his friend with excessive laughter and by ordering drinks for all present. Finally, he was able to sell everybody the idea that Alvin and Valerie had had a thing going. Valerie had run away when she had discovered that she was pregnant with Alvin's baby, Luther told them.

"Is dat why him wife lef' him you know," he told Meg.

She was surprised to hear it. Meg was the barmaid at Chance's Saloon.

"Yes," Luther continued. "You rememba say is not long afta him wife lef' him dat Valerie run way?"

"You right," Meg agreed. "Poor Alvin. Him lose two woman one time!"

Luther doubled over laughing. He slapped the stoned – out Alvin on the back.

"My man, Al!" he joked. "You tink him easy?"

Then he helped Alvin into his van and started to drive him home. As he drove, Luther chuckled, singing Alvin's song and adding his own words to it. This happened frequently, and in time Luther had made up his own song, which he sang as the drunken man lay snoring in the back of the vehicle. He looked in the back at Alvin one day and grinned.

"Tink a you one have talent?" Luther asked.

When Alvin heard the rumour his friend had started, he was hopping mad.

"Is what dat I hear say you a tell people 'bout mi?" Alvin asked.

"Eh?...Oh. You mean 'bout you an' Valerie?" Luther was laughing again.

"It no funny, man!" Alvin objected. "Is mad you a get mad or wha'? You well know say nutten don't go so. Inez leave mi because she didn't want to look 'bout Chad."

"Yes mi frien', me know dat."

"So wha' you a tell people lie fo'?"

"Is jus' a little joke, Al. You can't tek a joke?... I don't know wha' you a get bex 'bout?"

"I don't like bad name," Alvin complained.

"You worry too much," Luther observed. "An' you meck me nervous sometime. Especially when you start to sing 'bout Valerie."

"I don't even know when I a sing," Alvin confessed. "An' nutten not goin' happen because o' dat. Nobody else don't know. Is because you feel guilty 'bout what happen."

"Guilty?"

"Yes. Why you don't go an' unburden youself, Luta? I will back you up. It wasn't your fault. Den both a wi can feel comfortable again."

"It done happen a'ready," Luther said. "Me a'right. Is you not comfortable. An' one fine day you might jus' decide fi go sing to di police an' mash up my life!"

"No, man. Don't worry," Alvin said. "I tell you a'ready say I not talkin' an' I not goin' to."

"Is so I like to hear you talk!" Luther said gleefully. "I know I can depend on you, mi fren'."

Luther was happily whistling Alvin's song as the latter left for home. Everything would be alright, he told himself. Alvin was a drunken fool, but his sense of honour would keep him quiet. His secret was safe. Everything would turn out just fine. But this confidence was not to last.

Not many months later, Alvin came home late one night. He was drunker than usual. Chad helped him into bed and was about to fall asleep again, when he heard his father's voice. When he got to him, Alvin was sweating and talking incoherently. He was unable to make complete sense of what he was saying but the words "Valerie" and "Sorry" were repeated over and over.

Chad shook him awake.

"Pops. Wake up, Pops!"

"Valerie?" Alvin asked sleepily.

"No, is me Chad."

"Oh, Chad?"

"Yes. Who is Valerie?"

"Valerie?...Nobody. Go back to you bed."

"Nobody? Nobody! You tink I am a fool, Pop? I want to know who dis Valerie is?"

Alvin sat up and looked at his son.

"Dat is not something you need to worry about, son. Go back to yuh bed. You have to go to school tomorrow."

Chad turned to go. "It look like what people sayin' 'bout how you was keepin' a next woman wid my mom was true. Is you cause her to leave mi. Is you why I don't have any madda. You meck mi sick, Pops!" he said.

Alvin lay awake for hours after Chad stormed out of the room. He had always been troubled by his decision to keep Luther's ugly secret. How could a man live unaffected by such a terrible thing? Valerie had been no saint but at least she deserved a Christian burial. He could never forget the weeks following her disappearance. Her mother almost cried herself to death. Her father had put on a brave face. He was sure that Valerie would call before too long.

Alvin had been very nervous, but Luther seemed as calm as ever. He only wanted to be sure that Alvin wouldn't tell. Luther had called a pre-mix company to cast the foundation of the house, before calling the men back to work some days later. John Gooden had died waiting for a call from his daughter. His wife had since moved away to live with relatives in Trelawny.

Now he was losing Chad's respect. Losing his only child all because of evil concealed. That could not happen. Chad was all he had. He would have to find a way to convince Luther to do the right thing, Alvin decided. He would have to find a way to awaken the man's guilt so it would bite him on the conscience. Luther would then feel compelled to throw himself at the mercy of the authorities. Alvin felt sure they would be lenient with his friend. He would support Luther. It had all happened a long time ago and everybody made mistakes. But justice needed to be done. Mrs. Gooden deserved to know what happened to her daughter. He knew he would have no peace till that wicked thing he had helped to cover was exposed. He had to reach Luther for his own peace of mind as well as for Chad to know the truth.

He spoke to Luther the following day after work.

"You ever wonder how havin' a daughta would affect you life, Luta?"

"Well, my wife can't have any more children so me have to be contented wid my one boy."

"Me love mi boy too, but me wouldn't mind if me did have a girl pickney... like John Gooden."

"You comin' wid dat again ?" Luther asked.

"I not tryin' to upset you, man. Jus' listen to mi. You rememba dat rumour 'bout me an' Valerie?"

"How much time mi mus' tell you say it was a joke?" Luther was losing patience. "Nobody don't tek dat serious."

"Chad tek it serious, an' him believe is dat cause him mother to leave."

"Is time everybody forget 'bout dat foolishness now," Luther said. "Look how long it happen?"

"You realize say I still dream 'bout it?" Alvin asked him. "Up to las' night."

"Why?"

"How you mean, 'Why'? I can't help it. Nobody can help what dem dream."

"Look here, Alvin. Tek dat ting off you mine, man. Is full time now!"

"But it affecting Chad. I can't lose him, Luta." Alvin paused. Then he said, "I didn't know I would ever say dis to you, but if you don't tell you secret to somebody, I will have to…fi mi own sake, but especially fi Chad."

Luther looked him square in the eye. Alvin knew that look. It was the same look he had given Teacher Morris when she punished him for cheating in class. That night the teacher's car had mysteriously caught fire and was burnt beyond recognition. Luther never actually told him that he had done it, but he knew that Alvin knew that he had been the arsonist. At that moment, Alvin was very glad that he did not own a car.

"So you still want mi to confess?" Luther asked him.

"Yes. Dat is di only right ting to do. Nobody deserve what happen to Valerie. You have to set tings right, Luta."

"A'right."

"A'right? You mean you goin' confess after all?"

"Yes. I tink you right. I shoulda do it long time."

"T'ank you, mi frien'!" Alvin said happily. "T'ank you. Everyting goin' work out a'right. I bet say you won't even spen' one night a jail! You wi' see, man."

Luther watched him walk away. Alvin was born a fool and would die a fool. How could he expect that he would throw his life and freedom away over Valerie? Sure he had liked her but what would people think if they knew? Valerie would have done anything to please him, but when she got pregnant, things took a different turn. He was sure that would have caused a scandal. Joan would leave him.

He told the girl to get an abortion and gave her the money to get it done. He was working late at the site that night when she turned up. She told him that she wanted her baby and nothing he could say would make her change her mind. He had to act. He never thought killing somebody would be so easy. Her neck in his hands reminded him of a chicken he had once strangled for Sunday dinner. She had stopped breathing some time before Alvin had appeared. If Alvin had not come along, that part of his life would have been a closed book. It should have been over and done with long ago. Now this idiot wanted him to throw away the life he had worked so hard to acquire! Just to satisfy his stupid sense of justice. How dare he?

Alvin went to bed sober that night. He felt a calmness which he had not experienced in years. Luther was going to confess and justice would be done. Valerie would be vindicated, and things would be alright. He slept like a baby. Close to the approach of day, he dreamt about Valerie again. It was a beautiful dream. She was getting married. Himself, her mother and father, as well as several people in Lebanon were present and having a wonderful time.

Chad cooked him banana and mackerel the following morning. As they ate, he said to his son, "Is not everyting you hear you mus' believe you hear, Chad?"

"Yes, Pops. Sorry 'bout what I did say. I didn't mean to hurt you."

"I know dat, son."

As they continued to eat, an inexplicable sense of foreboding began to take hold of Alvin. It shadowed the morning like a heavy cloak of doom. Chad was about to leave when he called to him.

"Chad?"

"Yes, Pops."

"If a time should come when you in need an' I not there to help you, go to Luta Byles."

"Maas Luta?"

"Yes. Tell him say you know what happen to Valerie Gooden."

"What? But I don't know anyting 'bout any Val…"

"Rememba what mi sayin' to you, Chad. Tell Luta say you know all about Valerie."

"So how dat goin' to help me?"

"Don't worry 'bout dat. Jus' rememba what I tellin' you now."

"You feelin' sick, Pops?'

"No, Chad. Jus' a little bit down. Me soon a'right. Go on now."

"A'right. See you dis evening"

Minutes later Alvin left for work.

Joan Byles watched as her husband left that morning. He had left without eating, saying he had something important to do today. This was not like him, Joan thought. Luther loved his food. He had been restless all night and wouldn't tell her why. Something was up and she wanted to know what. She decided to follow him. Fortunately for her, his work site was very close to their home.

She was hiding among the tall blades of guinea grass when Alvin arrived.

"Hey, Al! You early man," Luther greeted him.

"Yes. How you dis morning, Luta?"

"Me a'right but Johnny say him have flu an' can't come today."

Joan clapped her hand over her mouth. That was so not true! She had heard Luther on the phone telling Johnny not to come to work that day, since he (Luther) had plans to go into town to buy work materials.

"But don't is Johnny suppose to do di roof work today?" she heard Alvin ask.

"Yes," Luther replied. "So is me an' you have to go do it now."

"But you know I don't like roof work, Luta. It meck mi kinda dizzy, man."

"Yes, but di work have to be done."

"Why you don't wait till Johnny feel …"

"You know say we workin' too slow on dis ting a'ready," Luther cut in. "Meck mi pour you a shot a dis whites fi steady you nerves."

Alvin could not resist the offer. He was beginning to think that his recent abstinence could be what was causing him to feel so gloomy.

"How you have liquor here so soon?" he asked, taking the glass.

Luther poured him a few more just to make sure. He had set things in motion from the night before. The beams of the upstairs house they were working on had just been set in place. So it was easy for him to replace a few of the solid pieces of wood with some which had long been rejected as rotten and useless. He was sure that they would hardly support the weight of a child.

"A'right," Alvin said. " I goin' try it now."

"Mi know you can do it, man," Luther encouraged. "Gwan up now," he said, pointing to the ladder which he had set in place.

Joan watched from her hiding place. She was getting bored. Everything seemed normal. Everybody knew how much Alvin liked liquor. Luther must have had a good reason for telling Johnny not to come. She was just about to leave when a frightening scream shattered the peace of the morning. It was Alvin's, and it was long, loud, terrible and fearsome. She watched, hardly believing her eyes, as Alvin's slender frame tumbled like a rag doll, the broken pieces of lumber from the roof under, above and around him. With a sickening final thud, his body hit the ground. Then all was silent. Joan was numb. She tried to move but she couldn't. She sat in the bush shivering, hoping desperately that this was a dream from which she was soon to awake.

She watched as Luther ran over to where the fallen man lay. He stooped down and looked closely at him. Without a word, Alvin drew his last, hollow breath and was still. Luther stood up and looked around him. Briskly, he set about moving the broken materials out of the way. Then he began to call for help. That was when his wife finally managed to drag herself away.

Alvin got a beautiful funeral. Luther paid for it. He made a great show of mourning his friend, telling everybody that it was Alvin's fault. The man had showed up drunk for work. He had warned him not to attempt to climb the ladder. If only Alvin had listened to him! He was in the middle of telling this story to one of their neighbours, when his eyes met Joan's. Abruptly, he stopped talking and asked to be excused.

Inez, who had since remarried, didn't attend the funeral, but Chad was a mess. Before he knew what was happening, Luther had rented out his father's house and moved him into his own. Steven was deliriously happy to have him, and Miss Joan could not have been nicer. She did all she could to make him feel welcome and comfortable.

It was a great house with all the food the boys could eat. Yet the tension between the man and woman could be cut with a knife. Steven told Chad that his mother had moved out of the master bedroom only days before he had come to live there. His father was sleeping alone these days. He had heard them arguing, but he had no idea what it was about.

The burial plot where Alvin's bones were interred was about a mile from what people still referred to as the "Lindsay house", beneath which Luther had buried Valerie. Mr. Lindsay had barely set foot in the house when he decided to pack up and leave again. He couldn't explain why, so the people of Lebanon concluded that life in England had affected his head. The house was sold for an excellent price to a realtor in Kingston who put it up for rent. It quickly lost its fame as the most beautiful house in the neighborhood and became known as the house with the most cantankerous residents in that town. Even quiet, decent people, who came to live there did not remain that way for long.

Shortly after Alvin's death, the owner decided to sell the house. He had had his fill of troublesome tenants. A valuator was sent to assess the place. Something was wrong, the man said. He couldn't put his finger on it, but something was definitely wrong. Luther challenged him on this so they went over the house together, foot by foot. Nothing seemed out of place. But instead of putting a price on the place, the man walked away without even collecting his fee.

Chad had, by this time, become an accepted part of the Byles household. The boys were in their third year at high school when Luther got the news that an engineer was being sent down to check the foundation of the Lindsay house. On this particular morning, Luther was unusually short-tempered and irritable. The family had just finished breakfast and he was getting up to leave. Steven had just rushed out to join some friends on a school trip and Chad could hear Miss Joan in the kitchen.

"Dad," Chad said. (Luther had told him to call him "Dad" and he felt compelled to do so, though the word tasted like gravel on his tongue.) "You rememba dat business me an' you was talkin' about?"

"What! Which business?"

"You say you would pay me to work wid you on Saturdays. Is three Saturday I been workin' now."

"Is money you a look dis mornin'?" Luther asked.

"Dem havin' a bicycle sale in town, an' I did want to buy one so…"

"You ungrateful you know, boy," Luther answered. "I tek you in, feed you, clothe you an' sen' you go a school an' now you a come ask mi to pay you!"

"But is you say you would pay mi."

"Why you don't give him that bicycle money out of what you collecting from Alvin house?"

Miss Joan had spoken. Chad didn't even know that she had been listening. She made a good point though, he thought. Luther was behaving like he was providing everything for him out of the generosity of his heart. Everybody in Lebanon knew that not a month went by when he did not collect rent from the tenants he had rented Alvin's house to. Chad never saw a cent of that money.

Luther turned angrily to face his wife and told her that it was none of her business. Then he strode out of the house. But Chad was a stubborn teenager who knew his rights and wanted his bike. The man was in the yard when he saw that the boy had followed him out.

"If you know what good fo' you," Luther threatened. "You woulda stop botherin mi 'bout dis foolishness. I have enough problem a'ready."

"Everybody but me have a bicycle," Chad complained. "An' is you did say you would pay mi to…"

Before he could finish, Luther turned in his tracks and slapped him hard across the face.

"Dat mus' shut you up now!" he fumed.

The blow stung like nothing Chad had ever felt before, but it was his pride which suffered most. He suddenly remembered his father. Had Alvin been here, Luther would never be treating him like this. But he was alone and at the mercy of this mean, cruel man. Then he remembered his last meal with his father and mumbled, "I know about Valerie Gooden."

He didn't think he had spoken loud enough for Luther to hear him but he had. He stopped and slowly turned to face the boy. Chad stared at him. Suddenly, he seemed like a different person. It was as though the man had shrunk before his eyes. Luther seemed beaten and afraid.

"So you daddy tell you 'bout dat?" he asked.

"Yes," Chad lied. He had no idea what he was talking about. All he knew was that people used to say that Valerie and his father had been involved. But if just telling him that he knew could make Luther so scared, this had to be something really huge. He was not about to let him know that he was just playing this thing by ear.

"What Alvin tell you?" Luther asked.

"You know an' I know," Chad said with as much bravado as he could muster.

Luther sat heavily down on an old log in the yard.

"Dis ting will nevva finish," he said slowly. "How long it goin' to follow mi? I tired o' it now!" It was as if he was talking to himself. "I don't know why I did get mix up wid dat own-way gal in di firs' place." Then he remembered Chad and asked, "So what you goin to do 'bout what you know?"

"I don't know yet," Chad told him." All I want now is di money you promise mi."

Chad was amazed at himself. This must be the survival instinct kicking in, he figured. He had never dared to speak to an adult like this before.

"You tell anybody 'bout what Alvin tell you?" Luther asked.

"No. Pop say it was a secret."

"Good," Luther said, getting up. "You wi get di money when mi come home dis evening."

Chad could hardly believe it. It had worked! Then he wondered again what all the fuss over Valerie Gooden was really about. Not that he really cared. All he wanted was his bicycle.

Later that evening, Luther sent Steven to his room and called Chad. He gave him the money and invited him to have a drink with him.

"What!" Chad was more than a little surprised.

"Don't you an' Steven is di same age?" Luther asked.

"I am three months older," Chad said proudly.

"Well I did give him a drink on him las' birthday."

"My dad wouldn't give me one drop," said Chad as he took the glass.

"Dat was when you was a little boy," Luther said, grinning. "Now you a big man workin' you own money an' ting!" He laughed cheerfully and Chad tried to join in. Then he asked, "So what you did say you goin' do wid you money?"

"Buy mi bicycle," Chad replied.

"Good. Sorry 'bout what happen dis mawnin?" Luther said.

Chad nodded his forgiveness as he tried to get used to the sting of the liquor in his mouth.

"I didn't even rememba say I did owe you," Luther continued. "You doin' a'right man. You soon move on to even hotter tings," he said, laughing heartily.

Chad was having a wonderful time. Now he knew why his father liked liquor so much.

Joan Byles listened from her bed to her husband's laughter. His love of life was the first thing that had attracted her to him. But she had lived with him long enough to know that he had the ability to laugh even when a situation was deadly serious and laughter was completely out of place. Her parents had been totally against their union. On her wedding day, her father told her to never take her eyes off Luther. When he died some years ago, he had left her enough money to take care of herself, in case her "pretty husband should turn ugly".

He had. Ever since the day Alvin died. Luther had sworn to her that he had nothing to do with Alvin's death. He had not known that the lumber on the roof was bad till it had broken under the man. He had taken it out of the way just in case anybody should try to blame him for what happened.

Joan was not convinced. They had not shared a bed since, and his attitude toward her had become distant and, lately, even offensive. She was happy that he had taken in Chad until she realized that he had done so because he wanted to collect money off Alvin's house. He was just not being fair to the boy. She couldn't help but wonder if Luther's maltreatment of Chad had anything to do with what might have happened between himself and Alvin.

It was past twelve o'clock when Luther felt sure that Chad was too drunk to know or care about what was happening. But he had to be careful, Luther told himself. He had to make sure his wife was asleep so she wouldn't try to interrupt his plans. He headed for her room, taking the stairs two at a time. Stealthily, he opened the door and tiptoed over to her bed. In the darkness, he stood over Joan and listened to her soft, measured breathing. He called her name twice just to make sure. No response. She was asleep alright. Likely under the influence of one of those sleeping pills she had recently started taking. She wouldn't wake up till morning, he felt sure. Luther left as quietly as he had come.

Back downstairs, he collected his cigarette lighter and some matches and went to get Chad. As he looked at the sleeping boy, a fleeting memory of himself and Alvin as boys came to his mind. Quickly he dismissed it. This was no time for sentiment. Deftly, he picked the boy up and swung him across his shoulders. Chad muttered something unintelligible and was quiet again. Luther headed for the Lindsay house. He would kill two birds with the same stone, he told himself. His problems would literally go up in flames tonight. The engineer who was coming to check the house might not even find Valerie's bones, and if he did, only Chad would know that Luther had put her there. But he was taking no chances. This thing had been following him for too long. Tonight it would all be over, once and for all. This boy snoring on his shoulders would be joining his father tonight.

Luther had been at the house earlier and had already doused it with gasoline. He would simply tell everybody that Chad had run away after he had scolded him about drinking. His wife had heard the boy sassing him that same morning, he would tell them. He had tried to be a father to the boy, but all Chad had wanted was to turn into a drunk like his father.

Luther would have been surprised to know that his wife was actually awake at that time of the night. He would have been angry to learn that she had only been pretending to be asleep. Joan had been very negatively affected by Alvin's death. She had been compelled to spend more time resting since then. If he had looked back as he left the house with Chad, he would probably have seen her watching him from her bedroom window.

After she saw him leave, Joan stood still for a moment. She remembered the argument between Luther and Chad the morning before. What was he planning to do to the boy? The memory of Alvin's death came flooding into her mind like a powerful, dirty river during rain season. She sat on the bed to steady herself. She was now fairly sure that Luther had murdered Alvin. Then she roused herself and ran to Steven's room. She shook him awake.

"Is what?" Steven asked sleepily.

"You dad gone down the road with Chad. I want you to follow him."

"Why?"

"I believe him going to hurt Chad."

"What!" Steven did not believe her. "Why would Dad want to hurt him?"

"Is a long story, Steve, an' I don't even know all of it."

"But why you believe Dad would want to hurt Bug Eye?" He looked closely at his mother. "You sure you a'right, Mom?"

"This is no dream, Steven," Joan said urgently. "I can't explain it now. Jus' run an' catch up with them now! I soon come."

"A'right," Steven said reluctantly. "But I don't even know where to go."

"I jus' tell you him head off down our road. Hurry up an' go on now before you lose them!"

"Yes, Mom."

Steven saw the smoke before he saw them. He was puzzled. Who could be burning garbage at the Lindsay house at this time? The house was supposed to be vacant.

He might as well check it out. He didn't even know exactly where he was supposed to go. His mother's nerves must be troubling her again but he had to humour her. As he neared the scene, Steven saw the shape of a man in the light of the first flames. He broke into a run. Then he saw that the man was his father. Luther was grinning. In the fire light, he resembled a crazy, yellow devil.

"Dad!" Steven called. "Where is Bug Eye?

"Steven?"

"Yes, Dad. Where is Chad?"

"What you doin' here?" Luther demanded. "Go home!"

"What you do wid Chad?" Steven asked again. "Mom say you leave home wid him."

"Go on home mi tell you!" Luther said, moving menacingly toward his son.

The boy moved to avoid him and fell close to the burning house.

"Is bun you want bun up to?" Luther asked.

"Bun up to?...You mean Chad inside di house? In di fire?..." Steven ran toward the entrance to the house. "Bug Eye!... Chad!" he yelled, running into the burning house.

"Steven, you mad?" Luther shouted, following his son into the house. "Come back!"

"Where you is, Bug Eye?" Steven kept calling. "Talk up, man! Chad Burrows, ansa mi! Help me to find you!"

Chad felt the heat and was thinking that Fatty had locked the room window and turned off the fan again just to mess with him. Maybe he should get up and open the window. The room was so hot! But he felt so tired.

"Say something Chad!" Steven called again.

"Shut up, Fatty!" Chad said vaguely.

"Bugs!' Steven called. "Is you dat? I comin' to get you... Don't worry. I goin' get you out o' dis!"

Luther was not far behind Steven, but neither was discernable to the other. It was dark and the smoke was getting thicker.

"Steven!" Luther was shouting. "Get out o' here now! You want dead inna dis fire?"

Steven ignored him and kept searching for Chad.

He found him shortly after he heard his friend mutter, "You wait till I wake up, man!"

As he took hold of Chad, Steven heard his father shout, "No, no, no! Dis can't finish like dis! It not suppose to done like dis! Help mi, Steve, Help mi!," Luther shouted.

A part of the building had collapsed on top of him. Steven was half-dragging half-carrying Chad to safety.

"Soon come, Daddy!" the boy yelled. "I jus' goin' get Chad outside...Soon come back fo' you."

The boys got out safely. Steven was about to return for his father when the Lindsay house caved in over its builder. Flames licked hungrily at the once majestic walls. People screamed and shouted. Women cried as the men made futile attempts to quell the fire with water, dirt and branches from the trees of Lebanon. Somebody ran to call the fire truck. Luther Byles should have been dead by then but he wasn't. By some force of good or evil, he was compelled to stay alive until his terrible story was told. All present were chilled into disbelief as he uttered his confession.

"Valerie, you hol' mi now!...Whai!" they heard him say. He was laughing and crying like a maniac. "'Bout you pregnant fo' me…You want mash up mi life?…Me pop you neck firs'!…Ha-haa!…You an' Alvin want mash up mi life?… I fix unoo business!…Ha-haa!"

A shout went up from the crowd as something exploded in the back of the burning building. Luther seemed unaffected. He continued his tirade.

"You get you revenge tonight, Valerie!…Whai!…You an' you killa inna di same grave tonight!…Ha-haa!…I comin' to you Valerie!…Mi a come, gal…Mi a come to you an' mi baby!…Wha hoo!.. Alvin, mi sorry!…Mi sorry fi haffi kill you, mi frien!.. But wi goin' meet back tonight, right?…Ha-haa!…Lawd God!…Wait fi mi, Alvin!… Wait fi mi, Valerie!…Wait fi mi, mi little baby!…Whai!"

The crowd was quiet. Only the bursting noises and the crackling flames interrupted Luther. Everybody wanted him to stop. To just shut up and die. If not for his own sake, but for that of his family. But they didn't move, and Luther was still not done. His voice was getting weaker, but they heard him clearly as he sang Alvin's song. Same tune but different words:

Valerie nuh want kill him baby
So Luta kill off di likkle lady
Oh, Valerie Gooden!
Valerie bury unda Lindsay house
Alvin a pass an' him find it out
Oh, Valerie Gooden!

Joan Byles fainted at this point and had to be taken away. Chad was beginning to come to. He kept asking for Steven who was nowhere in sight. Chad was among the

onlookers who heard Luther for the last time. Faintly he
sang:

Alvin a sing when him drink him rum
Luta a wish say di man did dumb
Oh, Valerie Gooden!
Luta tell him fi shut him mout'
Alvin say him a go shout it out
Oh, Valerie Gooden!

His voice was barely audible now. The crowd was
quiet, a tense, awful kind of quiet, straining with a mixture
of revulsion and curiosity, to hear Luther's final words:

Luta Byles kill Alvin dead
Chad Burrows watch you h____

That was it. Luther was finally silent. The people sighed,
exhausted and relieved. They continued watching as the
once mighty walls disappeared under the furious onslaught
of the hungry, darting flames. Most of the roof had, by then,
buckled in and had become one with the heavy, steaming
mass of charred metal, wood and smoke. As the sparks
flew dangerously closer, the crowd withdrew to a safer
distance. The efforts of the fire fighters seemed ridiculously
ineffective against the rage of the all-consuming fire.

This fire, started by Luther Byles, had turned on him
like a nemesis, vindicating Alvin, burning away the lies
which had clouded Valerie's disappearance and bringing
Luther's life to a shameful and bitter finish. Relentlessly, it
purged and uncovered as it went blazing, raving and
ravaging under the gloomy, smoke-filled skies of Lebanon.

Finally, fulfilled and satisfied with the vengeance it had wreaked, the fire yielded to the water.

Close to morning, the firemen completed cooling down operations. Joan, Chad, Steven, and almost everybody else had left by then. But that night would live forever in the memory of the people of Lebanon, driving sleep away for many more nights to come.

It was a double funeral. Lebanon was in a forgiving mood and everybody who could attend, did. The preacher was hard-pressed to find plausibly decent words in speaking of the life of Luther Byles but he managed. Valerie's mother was present. She was sad but grateful that the mystery of her daughter's disappearance had been finally solved. Mrs. Gooden hugged and consoled Joan Byles. There was not much to bury, but the formality of the memorial services brought a degree of closure to the events leading up to that terrible night.

The previous site of the Lindsay house now lies bare and abandoned, occupied only by hardened ash, black stones, bugs and lizards. Little children point to the spot as a place to stay away from since duppies live there. But an older, more experienced child might rebuke them for pointing, since such an act could cause the finger used in pointing to "rotten and drop off".

Steven and Chad are now grown men. They remain close friends but neither is in construction.

Joan Byles moved out of Lebanon shortly after the burial of her husband. She considers Chad as much her son as Steven and keeps in constant touch with them both. She is still plagued by the memories of the way Valerie, Alvin and Luther died, but the occupants of the small children's home she has started help greatly in keeping such thoughts at bay.

Inez was as perturbed as she was surprised when she finally met her adult son. Quickly, she dispensed with the business of meeting, greeting and sending him packing. She could not take the risk of being seen with Chad, since that would reveal to her friends that Inez had not only already traversed the highways of middle age, but was soon to make the bend into the descent to old age. But Inez is tough. She will fight this thing with all the weapons that the beauty shop can supply her.

Chad, who admires spunk, may find this the most appealing quality in his mother. That is, if he is not embarrassed by war paint.

THE LOVER

The first principal I can clearly remember is Mr. David Lawrence. He was a highly educated man. Everybody wondered why he had chosen to 'bury' himself in a place like Canterbury, our remote little mountain village.

Mr. Lawrence was a dark-skinned man of almost fifty. It was not his greatness of stature which made him such an imposing figure. He was short, and though not exactly stout, he had the clearly defined beginnings of a pot belly. His booming voice, piercing eyes and brooding countenance terrified me and his other students. Mr. Lawrence had a plump wife and a skinny little son. The child was his idol and he spoiled him rotten.

That boy could bawl like a tormented ghost. Many times as Mr. Lawrence stood poised to level his strap on the back of an errant student, his mighty arm was stilled (or at least weakened) by an unexpected bellow from Mitchie. That was the boy's name. Mitchie. So while we never got close to Mitchie, we loved him for his earth shattering noises and the anguish they caused his father.

Mitchie and his mother and father occupied the two-bedroom teacher's cottage, which stood a few yards away from the long single-room schoolhouse. This room was separated into different classes by large blackboards. The larger of the room's two entrances opened on to a dusty porch. It was the door to this porch that marked the division between the upper and lower school.

Generally, only senior students were allowed on the porch, and this privilege they guarded fiercely. Any junior person who wandered on to the porch would be promptly escorted off by an alert older child. During the first few weeks after promotion to upper school, seniors were usually so overcome by their own personal achievement that they were literally dumb struck. For long periods they would stand in silence on the porch, gazing in awe at one another.

Mr. Lawrence loved his plump wife. At that time, being fat was very stylish. Anybody who lost ten pounds or more had the sympathy or suffered the ridicule of everybody else, depending on whether that person was liked or disliked by the neighbours.

So the principal loved his wife. He also "loved" some of the teenage girls in his class. The fact that these children did not feel even slightly the same way toward him mattered not to Mr. Lawrence. His ploy was to ask the girls to do little chores at the cottage while his wife was away repeating subjects she had failed in her teaching examinations. (Some people felt that Mrs. Lawrence was not so bright.) While the girls resentfully did chores for him, this lecher would find some pretext on which to leave his class and go over to the cottage.

I believe it was Mr. Lawrence who first introduced sexual harassment to Canterbury. But this slackness could not go on forever. Indeed, it was to come to an embarrassing and violent end.

Paulette Mullings, a tall, beautiful black girl, was just beginning to blossom into womanhood. She was a senior in Mr. Lawrence's class. Paulette could be very sweet but she had a temper. Rumour had it that she once clobbered two lower school boys at the same time. Most of us liked her a lot and feared her a little.

Mr. Lawrence was always stealing glances at Paulette's chest. With head bowed in apparent concentration, she would pretend to be fully focused on her work and totally unaware of him. Then, as he stared, absorbed to the point of almost beginning to drool, she would look up suddenly, catch and hold his gaze with mockery in her own, while a scornful little smile played on her lips. Mr. Lawrence would come to himself with a start, noisily clear his throat while darting fleeting, uncomfortable glances around the class. His embarrassment would quickly turn to anger and then he would turn on us. We liked Paulette, but we were grateful that she did not come to school everyday.

This happened many times and I wonder now, as I did then, why a person as smart as our teacher did not learn to anticipate Paulette's responses and act to avoid his own unease.

Then the day came when Mr. Lawrence puckered up his courage to the sticking point and elected Paulette to go wash his dishes. As she flounced belligerently out of the class, he stared tiredly after her. We stared too. Then he collected himself and yelled at us to get on with the work. We pretended to write, peeking at him from below nervous eyelashes. Within a few minutes he shuffled out of the school. We were tense and quiet, listening hard.

Paulette was waiting for him. He howled like a wounded animal as the girl kicked him viciously in a place where no man should be kicked. Then she ran like the wind, leaving everything behind. Thus was Mr. Lawrence rendered (at least temporarily) impotent. He was out of our lives and on his back for two weeks. Paulette, who was subsequently transfered to another school; was the last girl to be asked to do chores at the cottage.

While we sniggered and gloated over his misfortune, many of us felt just a teeny bit sorry for the man. After all, he was our teacher. He knew his stuff. Many of us thought he knew everything while we and our parents knew nothing. So we hoped that this encounter with Paulette would somehow make him more accessible to us. We longed for peace with Mr. Lawrence.

But if hell holds no fury like a woman scorned, the same thing applied to a man scorned and beaten. Mr. Lawrence came back so angry that we could almost touch his rage. Now we were doubly afraid of him. Some of us were flogged, not because we did not know the answers to the questions he asked, but because, despite our overwhelming desire to speak, our lips remained as tight shut as those of the lions in the den with Daniel. School attendance dropped. Those who stayed away, secretly worried that Mr. Lawrence would come to their homes and flog them there. Something had to happen.

Mrs. Lawrence finally graduated from college and came to work by her husband's side. Half of his class became hers and she took over the running of the canteen. We had never suspected that she was a nice person.

Mrs. Lawrence had learnt at college that she should give stars and stickers to encourage her pupils, and she did. All the cowards who stayed home hiding behind phantom headaches, belly-aches and other anonymous medical problems longed for the incentives which the brave hearts who went (or were made to go) to school never stopped boasting about.

Unbelievable as it was, Mr. Lawrence changed a little for the better. Some people credited the change to the fact that the "higher-ups" had become totally opposed to the flogging of children, and the principal had been threatened with jail time unless he changed his wicked ways. Some said he had bad nerves, and now that his work load had been lessened, he could act more normally.

One day, in a bid to improve Friday school attendance, Mrs. Lawrence served fried dumplings and fish. After lunch, she announced that the menu for the coming Monday would be fried chicken and rice. All the faint hearts who were still clinging to their aches and pains became magically well that weekend. More than ninety per cent of the school's population was in attendance that Monday. The lunch turned out to be fried chicken back instead, but nobody had a problem with that. We were happy to be back to what was normal.

Mr. Lawrence was a lover of poetry. He even named the houses in school after famous English writers. (West Indian literature had not yet been introduced to many schools at the time.) I was in Wordsworth house. Shakespeare always won, and we always came last. Mrs. Lawrence, who eventually became the leader of our house, told us that we were not "being kind to poor Mr. Wordsworth at all" and that it was a "good thing that the poor man died!"

The following year our house came second. Mrs. Lawrence gave us so many goodies to eat that many of us became ill. Several doses of liver salts, antacid and other home remedies had to be administered to get us on the road to recovery from diverse digestive disturbances.

Mr. Lawrence exposed us to the grandeur of language in poems such as "The Solitary Reaper" and "Daffodils". His singing classes were his best. On Thursday afternoons, we were transported to the banks of "Sweet Afton" as she "flowed gently". Farmers coming from bush would stop to listen, remarking that Teacher Lawrence was doing okay. He even taught us folk songs. We sang of "Mi Coffee" and the beautiful Jamaican "Dry Yellow Yam". It was cricket season when he took us to Sabina Park.

The summer holidays were almost upon us when we heard that Mr. Lawrence would be leaving our school. This was very disturbing news, largely because we did not know how to react. We had become accustomed to fearing and resenting this man who had terrified us into acquiring knowledge we were now proud to have. We were confused at finding gratitude in our hearts.

"Missa Lawrence a go 'way!" was the buzz in Canterbury.

Many of us did not believe it at first. We had spent so long breaking Mr. Lawrence in. Or was it the other way around? Either way, it was as though he belonged with us now. But reality set in as the packing and preparations for moving began at the cottage.

"You goin' miss you teacha, Dove?" my grandmother asked.

"No!" I answered.

But my denial was too quick and too loud to ring true. Grandma peered closely at me over her spectacles. Then she smiled knowingly and shook her head. She did not believe me.

On the day he left our village, we were hiding in the bushes along the roadside. We watched as the big trucks took Mr. Lawrence and his family out of our lives forever. Many wept openly. Those who stubbornly refused to show regret found themselves incapable of hurling the many missiles (verbal and otherwise) which they had stockpiled for him.

Many years have passed since that day. Many more teachers have come and gone from Canterbury School, but the memories of Mr. Lawrence are still strong. We remember him with gratitude more than we do with trembling. A kinder judge may have seen such a man as one who strove valiantly to do the right thing. A man who wrestled daily against himself and who, therefore, might be forgiven for his indiscretions in the moments when his demons were victorious.

ABOUT THE AUTHOR

 Ditta Sylvester is a school teacher who has always enjoyed writing. She was educated at Dinthill Technical School and the Mico Teachers' College. She began to take her writing seriously after her first short story was published in *The Gleaner* in 2003. Since then, several of her stories have been published in Jamaica's leading newspapers.

Her awards include "Highly Commended" short story from the Commonwealth Broadcasting Corporation, gold and silver medals and a "Special Writer" prize from the Jamaica Cultural Development Corporation.

www.ingramcontent.com/pod-product-compliance
Lightning Source LLC
Chambersburg PA
CBHW050820180626
46814CB00004B/1378